Over The Ocean

Danielle Rohr

To Contact Wybear Press:

e-mail : wybearpres@aol.com

First Edition: Over the Ocean

Copyright©2014 by: Danielle Rohr, All Rights Reserved

ISBN-13: 978-0615947372 (Danielle\Rohr)

ISBN-10: 0615947379

Cover images: Lonesome Home, copyright©November 2013 by

Evergreen Turtle Studios:.All rights reserved

Interior Graphics: Evergreen Turtle Studios and Felix Desoto

Collaboration and Design by: Wybear Press and Danielle Rohr

For my Finch in the Big Easy

Table Des Matières

Un

"Jill, we have to run!" She shouts with urgency. Without looking back Mia bounds forward, dashing in between the walkers and cyclists.

Shadowing her, one girl after the other, Jill trails Mia through a maze of pedestrians. Only a quarter past seven in the morning and the buzz and movement of people flow through the streets. Paper cups full of steaming latte and designer bags bulging with the day's necessities are fastened to those who sweat productivity. Bums and students are a bit slower and cause a kink in the rhythm which jams up towards the end of the block.

Jill twists her arm behind her to steady her overstuffed backpack. She pushes on, trying to catch her runaway friend. No time to call out to wait. Jill knows she has to run. They somehow need to go faster than they can travel. They're late.

"There!" Mia shouts, looking back to give Jill an intense glance. She points at the BART sign. Light sprays off of the iron handrail which guides travelers who habitually descend into the deep hole.

The entrance is several minutes away. Mia turns willfully, bracing her arms, kicking into a full stride.

Jill lowers her head, sucks it up and pushes herself forward. As she jogs her pack seems to counter each step, working to pull her back and slow her momentum. She knows she's not going to catch up, but resigns to doing her best and eventually she reaches the station.

Compressed by schedules they continue down the concrete steps just below the heart of the city. A long hollow tunnel that's much quieter and more formal than the streets above provides a place of transition, the beginning point where they'll take the first leap.

The women insert their crumpled dollars into a futuristic terminal, which in return gives little tickets with arrows that seem to point them further in the direction that they need to go, but, more importantly, in the time they need to be there. A slight glimmer of progress spreads across Mia's worried expression. The high speed train pulls to a stop. The automated doors open.

Like the night before when they explored Berkley, this morning; Mia leads the charge. She selects a car near the front. Jill steps in pace behind her. When the women take their seats, they sit rigid and sideways. Jill studies the sign that illustrates all the points between Berkley and the San Francisco International Airport. She counts each stop and wishes there were fewer. The trip of a lifetime; the biggest trip either woman has ever imagined and they over slept.

"Hi." A young man with an oversized shirt and a neon blue hat interrupts their focus. He squeezes into the seat across from the hesitant women.

Jill and Mia pause to greet him. His effort to say hello is suspicious. Everyone else in the stuffed train-car works hard to shift their eyes away from any hint of acknowledgment. His greeting crosses over some underlying transit etiquette. His abnormality creates tension. He turns his knees in their direction, his hips follow. He's now impossible to avoid.

"Nice backpacks. Are you going on a trip?" He smiles and gives the women a lingering glare that's too familiar for Mia's comfort.

Mia lowers her head and lifts her gaze to stare him down, unhindered by his forwardness. "Yes." She gives him a hard look which causes him to inch back in his seat. She says no more. This silences the intrusive passenger.

Jill turns away, using her eyes to regard the figures who are nestled into seats patiently awaiting the start of yet another over-stimulating day. She looks at Mia who smiles briefly before casting her eyes above the crowd, focusing on nothing specific. She tries to do the same; however, the friendly young man notices her openness and tries to initiate another conversation.

"Are you going to Missouri?"

Jill cocks her eyes to the side, trying not to move her head as she looks at him. "Huh?"

"Missouri!" He doesn't elaborate.

Mia leans across Jill and shuts him down. "No."

"That's cool. That's cool though. You ever been to Missouri?"

Jill can't help herself; she looks at Mia then starts to laugh. The man in the neon hat laughs too.

"Aaaah, girl, you know what I mean. You get me." He grins at Jill. She tries her best to not get caught in an unwanted conversation. She doesn't get him, but his mannerism isn't threatening, and all he wants is to say hello.

Jill decides to give him courtesy. "So are you from Missouri? Are there lots of backpackers there?"

He raises his arms and folds his hands behind his head in a slouching stretch. "What? Aaaah, no. I've never been there."

He starts to laugh again. The joke evades her but the absurdity does not. She giggles from his silly question and from the joy to be in route to their big adventure.

"Well, my stop is coming up here in a minute."

He rises from his seat, holding the divider for balance while the train slows. He looks at the women, then at his daypack. He pulls something out from the side pocket of the gold zippered bag. Jill peeks from the corners of her eyes. He has a crumpled up brown bag. He moves closer to her. Panic settles its way into her thinking process. He stands right in front of Jill. Her eyes are now level with his crotch. She tries to look down. He holds out his hand, crinkling the brown bag with its mysterious contents.

"Do you like skunk?" He whispers over the hum of the train cars and the movement of passengers.

"Uhhh, yes?" Jill can barely hear him, but decides it's better to comply with whatever he's trying to ask her."

The BART stops. Jill and Mia's nerves calm.

The young man shoves the bag into Jill's lap. "For your trip."

He's enveloped by a surging crowd before he disappears from the train. Mia stares in horror at the bag resting on Jill's lap. Jill snatches it up and tucks it down by her side.

"Woah! What is that?" Mia demands.

Jill leans into Mia's ear. "He said it was skunk."

"What?" Mia's eyes narrow with confusion.

Jill whispers one word very slowly, "Drugs."

"You're serious? We can't take that to the airport. He probably thinks you're a drug mule or something. I can't believe you took that from him! Jill, next time; don't talk to anyone on the BART! I'll handle the weirdos."

Jill looks down in distress. She's also a little thrilled and impressed with herself because a strange guy just gave her a bag full of skunk. "Don't worry, I'll get rid of it." She answers coolly, happy to be the holder of the forbidden substance, ready to deal with her new predicament.

"It's not that simple, Jill. The BART is littered with video surveillance and so is the airport. You know, the *International* Airport!" Mia shakes her head, stressing over her friend's poor judgment. "I'm late, and all we need is to be detained by security. Get rid of it!", she growls.

Jill squeezes the crinkled brown bag in her hand, pondering the possibilities within. She could sell it and use the money for their trip. She could try some to make the flight more interesting. She could throw it in the trash at the next stop. She wonders if Missouri is some sort of special code and he gave the drugs to the wrong women. What if he discovers his mistake and comes after them? She deduces the best option is to ditch the skunk. She flexes her toes in her shoes and tries to relax for the final link to the airport. For now, she feels entirely interesting.

.   .   .

Last night was a wonderful celebration, marking the beginning of an adventure that Mia and Jill have been planning for several months. Mia arranged for the two to spend the night at a friend's dorm near UC Berkley. Her name is Royal and she was happy to give them the grand tour of the local eateries and colorful street characters. Unfortunately, it seems Mia and Jill enjoyed themselves too much, since this morning they failed to meet the day at the necessary time to get Mia to her flight.

The two friends planned, then unplanned, imagined, scheduled and dreamed their trip. With all the details and an uncommitted approach, it turns out that they ended up booking different flights. Mia's flight is first, and is scheduled to leave a quarter past eight in the morning. Her flight will have a layover in Chicago before heading directly to their first place of business: Amsterdam. Jill's flight leaves an hour and a quarter past Mia's, and will go abroad immediately with a layover in Germany. They have three more stops and a little over an hour to burn.

"Jill, I'm going to miss my flight. I'm not going to get to go. What am I going to do?" Mia looks crushed. All the color is draining from her usual bronzed complexion. She stares with misery at the map, measuring the distance between herself and the airport. "I'm screwed, completely screwed".

Jill can see the acceptance of defeat smother the spark of brilliance that's been filling their dreams for so many months. Just like her mother, Jill sides with the slim slice of hope still flailing about. "We're going to make it. Here look at what time it is." Jill holds up her cell phone. Still, the clock ticks on and minutes are lost.

"Did the train just slow down? Do you feel that? I think we're slowing down."

Jill smiles affectionately at her friend.

Mia shakes her head and looks back at the simplistic route of the subway. Jill slides in closer beside her friend, kicking the enormous backpack a little closer as she goes. "Your flight isn't taking off for another hour and fifteen minutes. You still have a chance. We'll get there. Just relax."

Words that are meant to comfort, but truly mean nothing are rambling from Jill. She knows they offer no real help, but right then, it's all she can think to do for her friend. Secretly in the back of Jill's mind she's smug, feeling grateful for the knowledge that she will easily make her own flight and with time to spare.

The steel chorus of the train rattles and races through darkness as it speeds from stop to stop. People empty out of the strange yellow train cars while new passenger's board, greeting the women with an aversion of their eyes and a lack of interest for where they are. Jill likes the fact that the passengers keep their eyes on their phones and tablets, or simply closed to rest during transport. This allows her to stare and observe them. She watches the people; these bay area locals who come and go around San Francisco. They're so different compared to the people back home in the valley, which is only an hour away. They're so fancy, so suave with eco-friendly brief cases or one-shouldered messenger bags. Everyone seems to be in drab earth-toned colors aside from their brightly painted hair and jewelry.

Mia taps her foot, mimicking the local passengers. She keeps her eyes down, shielding out the things that might temper her impatience. Jill has her arm over the top of the seat while leaning in towards her friend, lost in thoughts that seem to be caught in a loop. The same questions and concerns cycle through her head with no solution until they actually arrive at the airport.

.　　.　　.　　.　　.　　.

Out of the tunnel and into the light of day, the train grinds forward and soon reaches the airport. In anticipation; Mia and Jill have their packs hugged tightly to their bodies. Plane tickets, passports, and identification are ready in hand. The train stops. The doors slide open. Like before, they find a speedy gait and rush down halls to extinguish their final distance. Mia halts to a stop before approaching the woman at the airline reception area.

"There's my flight Jill!" She points a stiff finger at the sign that lists arrivals and departures. The plane is still there. She has forty five minutes. "We made it. You get rid of your drugs! I'll go check in."

Jill nods her head discretely, scanning the open space of the terminal. She inspects the ceiling, spying for security cameras. The crumpled bag of skunk is shoved deep into her pocket. She slides her hand down, gripping the contraband. She steps away, following the walls until they take her to a bathroom. She scopes out her exit. Looking left, then right, and lastly behind her. She pulls on the door handle and slips inside, spy-style. She tries hard not to skip into the bathroom stall, but her feet can't help but feel light. In her deepest heart, she's delighted to have been given the impulsive drugs. She thinks about it: what if she takes some and throws out the rest? She wants something fresh and different. She reasons she'll try just a little, then to appease Mia, she'll throw away the rest. Right down the toilet. Her hand feels hot and shaky; she pulls the paper bag up, dragging it past her thigh slow and deliberate. She's quiet, forgetting to breathe. The bag is free. She lifts it closer to her face for inspection. She stops, listening to the empty bathroom, preparing to react if someone might catch her. She pinches the opening and pulls it apart. The paper is less crinkly and crisp, it's now more smooth and supple. It's dark inside the bag, but she can see shreds and pieces of something.

"Skunk, it must be some kind of marijuana, perhaps hashish or something. I'll just try to take a pinch and swallow it whole. I'm sure I'll feel the effects. Mia would be so mad at me. Then she'll laugh at me".

She spreads the opening a little wider, then holds it back so the fluorescent light washes in. She squints her eyes, and realizes it isn't hashish.

Oh.

She peers into the bag, eyes bigger and full of disappointment.

Scones.

She sniffs. *"Blueberry Scones. He must have said scone, not skunk".*

Jill turns and tips her paper bag up-side-down, emptying the crumbles of pastry into the toilet bowl. She shrugs before dropping the entire bag into the porcelain abyss. She reaches out listlessly and in a final flush, parts ways with her brief fantasy.

Meanwhile, Mia rushes the desk, there are no lines to wait in. She's skilled when it comes to speaking directly and communicating what she wants. She takes a breath, makes firm eye contact, and as simply as she can explains to the woman; "I need to be on this flight," she holds out her neatly folded paper ticket. "The plane is about to leave. Can you have it wait for me?"

She lifts her navy blue backpack onto the big scale that divides the airline counter. The woman's eyes widen as she reviews which flight Mia demands. Mia can't read the woman at the counter's expression. The woman is good at shielding her intentions from the customers. She reads the ticket a second time, then addresses Mia. Jill lingers off to the side. She sets her pack on the floor and resumes her role as Mia's shadow.

The woman finally locks eyes with Mia and prepares to explain their fate. "Ms. Juarez, let me call about your flight." The poised airline clerk in a form-fitting vest lifts the phone to her ear. The nervous friends watch the white coils of the cord stretch then compress as she pulls the receiver closer to her ear.

Mia and Jill both know what will happen next. The woman will get off the phone and announce they are going to get Mia on her plane while pinning an express tag to her luggage.

With little empathy, the woman states that Mia is at the front desk and needs to board the plane. They watch intensely. Whatever is being said is unreadable to the uneasy travelers.

The airline representative silently sets the phone back on its vertical cradle, then locks eyes with Mia. The woman squares her shoulders and begins a short, confusing apology. "Ms. Juarez, we are so sorry, but your flight is boarding right now. In your ticket, here," she waves to a portion of the small home-printed ticket. "Your ticket requires that you check in at least an hour and a half before your flight's departure. Unfortunately, you're too late to ride on this flight. I'm so sorry, Ms. Juarez."

Mia boldly places her small hand on the counter. "What? How can you just not let me on the flight? I'm here and the plane hasn't left yet. I paid a lot of money for this ticket. It's non-refundable." The strength in her tone cracks. "What do I do?" Tears start to fill up the pockets beneath her green eyes and heat flushes her reddening face. "Can you refund my money? Can I get on another flight?"

The airline representative gives the devastated travelers a more human look. "Here at this desk, I can only check in customers. If you'd like to discuss the possibility of another flight or a refund, you can use our complimentary guest service phones over there." She holds out a long manicured finger that points to several black phones bolted to the wall opposite of the counter. Mia starts to shake, trying to control her anger at the woman, the situation, and her own poor choices.

Jill steps forward and grabs Mia's hand, "Let's go," Jill scoops up her pack, then drags Mia's behind her.

The archaic black courtesy phones can't help but threaten a warning of doom. They are unmistakably "the end of the line". These are the grim last chances; sentinels of terrible news. Anyone who finds themselves in the position of having to use them is screwed. Mia steadies her hand to dial the 1-800 number on the faded keys of the number pad. She's connected and begins to explain her situation. She's put on hold, then she's told to go back to the counter. They are going to get her on the flight if she can go right now.

In a blur of checking in and running down halls through terminals, Mia reaches her gate. It's closed and another woman adornrd by the same form-fitting vest informs them, "You didn't make it."

"But I'm here. There's the plane. Let me on!" Mia feels dizzy from the airport ping-pong stress.

"I understand, honey, the problem isn't with you. Your luggage is going through screening because you are heading for an international flight. I know it sounds unreasonable, but the fact is: you . . . didn't make this flight. What you can do is call our customer service and try to get on another flight."

In the longest ten minutes of Mia's life she finds herself in a blur of skating several times back and forth between customer service airline phones, and an airline counter. At one point Jill is on the phone with the airline, while Mia's talking to an actual customer service representative at a desk. But, with their prayers, divine intervention occurs. A very nice and less complicated voice on the phone sincerely listens to Jill explain their dire situation. Jill clears her throat and forces herself to slow her speech despite the dwindling time constraint. "Hi, my name is Jill Tulver, and I have a flight that is scheduled to leave for Amsterdam in two hours. I'm leaving on a trip with my friend who has a different flight. We reached the airport late. The plane hasn't left yet, but we are being told we won't be able to board her on her flight. Is there any way you can get her on my flight?"

Jill did it. She communicated as clearly as she ever had, precisely what they need. To her surprise the voice doesn't reject.

"So, Miss Tulver, I'm looking at your flight. Oh, uh huh, I can see the flight your friend is going to miss. It hasn't left yet. Hold on, I'll see what I can do."

Jill held on, not speaking or breathing, not even moving, purely waiting and holding.

"Miss Tulver, your friend, Mia Jaurez? I just booked her a seat next to you on your flight. I hope that helps. Have a wonderful trip."

Jill can hear the agent's smile through the phone. She somehow has a mental block around what the customer service rep has instructed. "Umm, so she doesn't need to do anything? Do we have to pay? Really, she's in a seat next to me?"

The voice on the phone giggles. "You're all taken care of. Just take Miss Juarez to the international check in so they can screen her luggage. You're both all set."

"Thank you!" Jill slams the obnoxious black phone back onto its cradle and starts to dance a victory jig. She shouts across the terminal, "It's arranged Mia, you're coming with me! No charge!"

"No way! That just doesn't happen!" Mia starts to tear up with happiness. The shock and relief from the blessed news cause the women to collapse in a heap on the floor of the airport with their carry-on's tossed carelessly beside them. For the first time this morning they can relax, and look ahead to the good flight bound for Frankfurt.

"Well, Jill, we have one hour before we board our flight." Mia grins at Jill with zest and humor. She laughs, again. "How does your happy-go-lucky ass do that? Only you, Jill." She shakes her head in awe of the effortless way her companion floats through time and space.

Jill's been waiting for Mia to pull back on the reins, to slow down her rushed pace. Jill wants coffee and food, and possibly a minute to wash her face before they settle into the jet plane. She knows with Mia it's better to be patient and wait for appropriate opportunities to address her humble personal needs. Jill's close to twenty pounds overweight, while Mia could be considered underweight despite her athletic physique. While Jill likes to eat and enjoy food, Mia seems to find making time for meals burdensome and prefers to run on pure energy; only stopping to eat when it's for the purpose of refueling. Jill enjoys rich flavors and textures, while Mia respects a food's ability to provide her with nutrients.

"Mia, let's go find some coffee and a muffin," Jill suggests. The whole morning has been about handling Mia's needs, and it is now time to address one of her own, When it comes to eating, the one common ground between the women is their mutual fondness for coffee and beer. They intend to enjoy both on this trip.

"I think I saw a Seattle's Best Coffee shop on the way to our gate. We have to leave this section and find the international flights." Just saying the words "The international flights." makes Jill smile in a way that makes her look so beautiful. They're now transformed into two very interesting people. More interesting than they were, because, now; they are single-young, international jet-setters. Eventually they find coffee, a couple of warm muffins and a bathroom.

While the two sit and wait to board the plane; Mia tries to coach Jill in preparation for Europe. Mia gives Jill a concerned look as her gaze climbs from her shoes all the way up to Jill's hair, which is fastened into a floppy pony tail piled on the top of her head. Jill squirms as she endures the visual inspection from her friend. Jill's wearing an old, too-tight pair of jeans, her sandals, and a surfer sweatshirt. Mia has on a pair of gray low-rise slacks with a button-down silk shirt, and cardigan. She wears European looking clogs that add height and glide silently across the airport tile. Mia has a special way of honestly and helpfully coaching her friends and family. Jill knows a criticism is coming, but this never really bothers her.

"So Jill . . . In Paris, I really don't want to look like a tourist." She gives Jill a gentle half smile, directing her eyes to Jill's jeans. "I did some research and I really want to blend in and look like a local. You know, dress and act the way the locals do. In Paris, women are a little more into fashion and really don't wear jeans," Mia extends the word "jeans", before pausing to give her friend's pants a discriminating look.

Jill smiles and her mind revisits her plan to dress comfortably and practically as they travel. Just like Mia, Jill has her own plans and preparations when it comes to traveling abroad. However, Jill's priorities are nowhere near making "blending in" an objective. She replies to her friend, not in defense, but in an informative tone to share her efforts (which she's quite proud of), "Mia, check it out, I wore these pants because they're my oldest pants that really don't fit me well. Look, they have a couple holes in them. This way, when I get to Amsterdam, I can just throw them away. Less weight to carry in my backpack." Jill is so proud of her strategy. She's also proud of being a tourist. "So, our bags are full, you know, and we really have no idea if we'll be able to wash our clothes. Mia, I went to Wal-Mart and bought twelve pairs of the .99 cent underwear!"

Mia tries hard to tolerate the genuine way her friend sees life. She gives Jill a blank stare.

Jill raises her voice with pride, "I am going to throw away my panties every day! That way I don't have to pack around my dirty underwear for two weeks. Think how gross it would be to carry around two-week old underwear with me everywhere we go. Plus, this will make a bunch more room for me to buy lots of souvenirs to bring home to America!"

Mia grins, thankful for the way her nerdy friend can make her laugh. "That's really good Jill, but let's do our best to blend in when we get to Europe. Especially Paris. Did you bring any dresses or skirts?"

Jill sighs. They've had this conversation a few times before. "Yes, I brought two skirts and a dress with me."

Mia has to coax more information from Jill, "What about shoes?"

"I have these," Jill points to the Birkenstock sandals that cover her toes. "I also have a pair of black heels and a pair of running shoes. They're called 'Roos', Mia! I found them at the outlet store. They have pockets that zip on the sides of them. Pockets on my shoes, Mia!" Jill is thrilled to share her newly acquired shoe treasure. Her voice rises in excitement.

Mia nods, trying to calm her friend.

"You know, Mia; so I can carry my money or maybe my passport on the sides of my shoes to avoid getting robbed while we're traveling."

While Mia was researching how to fit in with the locals, Jill was researching fear-based concerns; like getting her passport and travelers checks stolen in a foreign country. Jill is certain they'll be victimized while exploring the world.

"I also have this," Jill whips out a strange little flesh-toned pocket on a cord that she's tucked under her clothing. "It's a traveler's undercover hidden pocket! I can keep all my money and documents in here and not have to worry about anyone stealing my purse or wallet!"

Mia sweetly nods her head, curious about the thoughts that run through her companions head.

Jill boasts "It's discrete and functional!"

Mia laughs. "Then it's the only discreet and functional thing about you, Jill!"

Jill replies "Uh, huh, just try to blend in my friend." She pats Mia on the shoulder. "While you're nervous and stressed in dark places, I'll be comfy and enjoying myself because my documents are safe and protected."

The paper cups of coffee are finished, then discarded. Jill brushes the carrot muffin crumbs from her very snug pants before stepping away from their morning perch.

Soon they board the plane bound for Frankfurt. As they squish into tightly rowed seats, they resign themselves to joy. What was only an innocent idea a few months ago is now actually happening. They are happening. All of the sudden, life shines a little more, destinations are mysterious. The world waits to be discovered.

"I can't believe we got you on my flight," Jill smiles, fishing for gratitude and wanting the credit for fixing the travel issue. Mia smiles even bigger. Simultaneously they both lean back into their seats. Basking in the glory, recalling all the work and circumstance that's lead up to this ultimate grip of what they are about to do.

.   .   .

It was back in February when Mia casually mentioned to Jill one day at work that she was planning a trip to Spain to visit her family, but was having trouble convincing her friends to accompany her. At twenty-two, everyone seemed locked down with jobs and school, or both. It was a dull, cold winter day at the Children's Museum. If anything Mia was just trying to brag, dream a little to a co-worker to pass the slow drip of minutes between the start of the work-day and the end of the seven hour shift. The museum is uneventful; most days they just monitor field trips, insuring that kids are respectful to the exhibits and don't run.

What Mia didn't know was that Jill needed a break from her life; which was feeling more constrictive than constructive. Jill was in the midst of a civilization course at the community college. She found herself leafing through her text book staring at photographs of sculptures and paintings that have been preserved for more years than she could comprehend. Jill was also taking a beginning painting course to satisfy her art requirement and she couldn't help but be completely affected by the timeless art featured in her professor's power point lectures. She wouldn't just admire the art, but she wanted to know who created it, when, and where. She spent hours thinking about how they made their own paint from minerals, stains, and imported materials.

Mia casually stood across a pathway in the museum opposite Jill. "I'll go to Europe with you."

Mia's green eyes flicker in response to the unexpected statement.

"You would?"

"Sure."

"You would just come with me? Jill, are you serious?"

With a daring smile that Mia had never seen before, Jill replies "Yeah, I'd be down for a trip to Europe, but I don't really want to go to Spain. What if we saw Paris, and then we split up when it's time to go see your family?"

"Yeah? I want to spend a month in Europe," Challenges Mia.

"I'll only do two weeks. I think I'd get homesick any longer." It is true, at twenty-four, Jill is a big homebody who still lives with her parents and younger brothers. She winks at Mia. "But, yeah, I'll go with you, Mia."

Mia and Jill were more co-workers than friends, only slightly compatible. It was Jill's confidence that made Mia realize she had found the perfect travel partner.

By March, they had purchased round-trip tickets to Amsterdam, which offered the cheapest airfare scheduled to fly out in May. In April, they purchased Euro-rail passes that encouraged them to visit as many countries as they could fit into the two weeks. Mia was generous and permitted Jill to pick the majority of the countries they would visit.

"I want to see the Matterhorn in Switzerland," negotiates Jill. "I want to see the Louvre in Paris," she insists like a greedy child.

Mia agrees, and as they explore more options with the internet, the trip begins to develop more complications. In the spirit of the backpacks they would be carrying; Jill found a campground on the outskirts of Amsterdam. Mia wasn't sure she liked the idea of a campground versus the fun of staying in an Amsterdam hostel. Jill promised they would have a better time and have more privacy near the outskirts of the city. She showed Mia how the campground is located on a beautiful river. Jill got her way and reserved a little primitive cabin at the campground. The only set back is that the cabin was twenty dollars more than a bed in the hostel. Money and expense are a big issue for the two girls, and they're trying their best to spend close to nothing on the trip.

.   .   .   .   .

May is finally here, and neither Mia nor Jill can believe they're actually going. The tight-fitting, long-sitting seats are okay. The airline food is cheerfully tasteful. The man that squeezes into their row is polite and handsome. Jill slouches into her seat and points her impatient legs straight beneath the seat in front of her. She stares out the window for so long. She looks at clouds. She looks at the way the light permeates and weaves through more clouds. She looks at the wings of the plane again and again, fascinated by the way the ice layers and collects around the edges. The sun rises, then sets, then it rises again, and they are still in the air, moving so far from anything familiar.

Jill rests in her seat and doesn't think of her friend beside her. She doesn't need to. Her companion is there, and would be there, throughout these explorations. She doesn't think about Europe. She's busy experiencing the flight, almost in a meditative state. She has a bladder built for travel and can sit undisturbed for quite some time.

While Jill stares and loses herself in thoughts of nothing but flying, Mia has her own methods for tolerating the long flight. A steady amount of trips to the bathroom and an iPod with naps suits her just fine. She's been shoved in the middle, sandwiched between the handsome man and Jill.

Soon the plane approaches Frankfurt.

Two bent, squished women try to unfold themselves from the strange ways the airplane seats form them. When they find a few chairs to spread out in to relax near the gate to their next flight, Jill pulls something out of her small backpack. Mia looks over, inquisitive and knows she will never guess what Jill has stowed in her swollen carryon. Her eyes grow round when hundreds of little seed beads roll out of a small clear container directly onto the flat part of an airport chair.

Jill expects to see a smile, but instead Mia gives her a troubled glance. Jill figures she owes Mia an explanation. "I brought beads to fill in the boring times like this layover." She pours more of the potpourri of rainbow colored glass across the seat of the airport chair. Next she settles into a yoga pose on the floor, before unravelling an elastic cord to tether the small jewels. "See, it's relaxing and I can make stuff to give to people we meet as we travel. It's a cool idea, yeah?"

Mia raises her eyebrow and moves herself away from her friend and the beads that are rolling around on the chair beside her. Jill isn't deterred by her friend's rejection of the beading. She happens to know Mia loves making beaded jewelry back home. Jill figures it's just one of Mia's moods.

Once, Jill catches Mia wince at the sound of several little glass seed beads sliding off the chair, hitting the floor, and rolling away to unforeseen places.

Again the women cowgirl up and find new seats on a much older, more European looking airplane. The inside of the airplane is orange and yellow, and, to Jill's amazement, the arm rests include built in ash trays.

"Can we smoke on the plane?" Jill asks Mia, pointing at the strange aluminum ashtrays.

"Well, we are going to Amsterdam!" Mia answers.

They both break into laughter.

Now in route to Amsterdam, the two are beginning to feel a little more deviant. Both Mia and Jill have had boyfriends who habitually smoked weed. It's ironic that it ends up being Mia and Jill getting to visit Amsterdam, and not their boyfriend counterparts who have Amsterdam tee-shirts, posters, and magazines.

Jill doesn't smoke anything. Mia smokes slightly more than that. The two girls didn't discuss the topic of smoking weed in Amsterdam, but it may be; each has their own itinerary regarding this activity. Perhaps that's what's making the trip so good. No expectations or projects appointed. Two empty baskets ready to be filled with experience.

The small plane reaches Amsterdam quickly. It's now sometime in the evening. Time has escaped the two travel companions and the only thing that guides their sense of day is the fading light that looks a little different on this side of the hemisphere.

Stumbling through corridors, the girls collect their backpacks. Strapping them over their shoulders, they leave the airport. Now walking through a train depot, they catch a shuttle that spits them out in the middle a central transit spot for the city.

"Oh, God! Mia, this is crazy; we're here!" Jill feels like throwing her pack down and doing an MC Hammer dance.

"We're where? Where are we Jill?" Mia starts pacing unintentionally. She takes two steps in one direction, then turns around and decides to go the other way.

"Look." Jill points to a friendly looking office building that could have been transplanted from Disney Land.

"Let's go." Jill takes Mia's hand and they jumble together up a long ramp which leads into some sort of visitor center. Inside all the information is in a completely different language than the dialect the women are used to.

"You know, Jill, I don't think we need to go in here. It's not in our language."

"What do you want to do then?"

"Let's find a taxi or bus or something to get us to the campground. I think it's going to get dark soon,"

The two nervous tourists go up a ramp, then back down. They hurry down a sidewalk to a bus shelter. Jill and Mia locate a colorful route map. It has the city divided into pale shades with small blue dots leading to stops. Mia struggles hard to interpret the map, considering each marking, hoping to decipher the unusual language. She stares harder, believing that if she looks with enough effort, she'll be able to decode the cryptic map. Jill rolls her shoulders allowing the heavy pack to fall from her back and slide to the ground. Then, without looking, she sits on top of all her belongings; tired and irritable from flying. Both Jill and Mia are confronted with the reality that they are going to have to figure out how to get around Europe. Jill notices a man who's just leaned his faded grey bicycle against the shelter. He's pulling out a cigarette from a little pouch mounted to his bike frame. Since the local looking stranger is close to Jill's age, she decides to ask him for help.

Jill reaches deep into the pit of herself to find the necessary courage she would need to ask for directions. Thoughts of doubt spread out like spider's webbing in her mind. One doubt connects to another, then leads on to more; a pattern of not wanting to leave her comfort zone. In California she would not, did not ask for help. Here, Jill wonders if it's even okay to walk up to strangers and ask for directions. What if this culture doesn't encourage strangers to converse? She stands and takes a breath, realizing her time is limited and the potentially helpful stranger is almost half way through his smoke break. Jill turns and observes her friend who seems to be trying to force herself to learn Dutch right there, right now on the street. The longer Mia stares at the map, the angrier and more annoyed she becomes. Jill knows she needs to intervene, get help, and bail out her ambitious sleep-deprived friend.

She stands up, pulling her pack along with her. In her tired and awkward efforts, Jill has captured the interest of several people milling about on the cobblestone sidewalk. She sets her sight on the guy, hoping that he'll be a savior, guiding them to the right bus. Jill drags her heavy bag along behind her, anticipating the criminal activity she's been imagining during all her months of preparation. The backpack resembles a dead animal carcass, limp and difficult to move. Jill resembles a wounded warrior, stiff and sore from a long battle and no sleep. The guy with the cigarette can't help but watch the strange girl who to his concern seems to be heading his way.

Jill watches him watch her. She is sorry for this, and wishes she were invisible. She struggles her way over to him. A little unnaturally, she tries to make herself look friendly and relaxed, but because these qualities are forced and far from genuine, her attempts translate into a disturbed, almost crazy-lady expression.

Jill realizes her own odd demeanor when the guy reaches for his bike and tilts it upright, so that it no longer leans on the shelter. He takes another drag from his sophisticated European cigarette. Jill knows Mia is watching too, and turns to catch a look of disapproval from her companion. Jill dismisses the judgment because it will just seem really weird if she bails on her mission now. Besides, Jill is going to actually accomplish something. It's up to her to find their way to the promise of the campground she had reserved many months ago.

Without a plan of what to say, she finds herself standing in front of the young man with the bicycle; her backpack stowed behind her. She smiles and uses her eyes to break down any prejudices he may have deduced while watching her advance towards him. He smiles and politely extinguishes the cigarette to give her his full attention. She puts her hand up in a strange wave like gesture. "Hi."

The man gives her a smile that isn't simply an invitation to ask for help, but a svelte and kind welcoming to his country. In his earnest look, Jill realizes that her preconceptions about a tough crowd and a rough city may be completely irrational. She wonders why she had ever suspected Europe to be unfriendly. Perhaps she won't fall prey to the possibility of becoming a tourist victim. With his smile she has permission to slow down and think of something to say.

"Hi," He tilts his bicycle away from his body and stands; giving her his full attention.

"Do you speak English?"

He laughs and places his other hand on the seat of his bike, leaning in. His laugh is loud and makes Jill feel a little intimidated. "I speak English. I also speak Dutch, German, and French. Can I help you with something?"

The man with the bike takes his eyes from Jill as they drift down to review her enormous backpack and then over to examine Mia who's obviously paired with Jill. He smiles again and politely waits for Jill's response. She doesn't, so he tries to help. "I like your hair. It's nice," he says with encouragement.

The comment derails Jill's focus and she stops to think for a minute what her hair might be like. She'd been on planes and a shuttle for so long that she hadn't really considered the state of her hair. Did he mean the lopsided frizzy ponytail? Did he like the brown color or the length? Jill lifts her hand to feel the hair on the top of her head. Aside from the frizz, it seems okay, even a little boring.

"Thanks." Jill hesitates and tries to think of something normal to say. "My friend and I just got here from America."

The bicycle man starts to grin, looking amused, but in a gentle way.

Jill is starting to feel at ease, accepting that he, she, and Mia all know she's a perfect disaster. She submits to allowing herself to ask for what she needs, deciding it doesn't matter what the bicycle guy thinks of her anyway.

"My friend and I are trying to find a campground."

The man's eyes crinkle at the corners as he thinks. He shakes his head, "There are no campgrounds around here. Are you sure that is what you are looking for?"

Jill isn't sure. She isn't sure of anything anymore. She isn't sure about the trip, or the campground, herself, and especially; she isn't sure of her hair.

She takes a step closer to the man, allowing the bicycle to divide the space between them. She holds out the tri-folded piece of printer paper she's pulled from her special travel pocket of documents. It has a few names of streets on a map and the reservation information. "Zeeburg?" she manages to say, feeling embarrassed for her vulnerability and the mispronunciation.

He holds the paper and starts to nod his head, which makes Jill and Mia feel a lot better. Mia slinks out from the bus shelter where she's been casually trying to hide. She slowly moves in the direction of Jill and the bicycle man, dragging her own pack like a burdensome friend. Mia wants to hear the information that the man is about to offer them.

The hint of burning tobacco drifts away on an evening breeze. The man leans over his bike, breaking down Jill's Americanized ideal of personal space. She likes it. He holds the paper out to her, and she takes one side.

Together, in a cozy sort of way, the two review her reservation paper. He begins to explain, and as he does, his voice softens and slows so that the girls can remember and understand.

"You want to get to this street. The bus can drop you off there. Look for a bus on the Yellow Line. Then you will have to walk down this street, at the end, turn right. You'll see a river. Cross the bridge that goes over the river. On the other side of the bridge is Zeeburg." Upon finishing his instructions he releases his hold of Jill's paper.

Jill turns to him and runs her hand across the top of her tired ponytail. She tries to smooth it in an effort to seem attractive.

"Thank you," she answers a little too loudly, trying to compensate for the fact that she's now a weird foreigner in someone else's country.

Jill and Mia notice the gold flecks in his amber eyes at the same time. They watch him lift his leg up and over to mount his bike. "You are welcome. Enjoy your trip girls." He pedals away without looking back.

Jill and Mia watch the stranger roll away on his bike, unhappy that they are alone once more, wishing for someone to figure it out for them. With nothing left to do, the girls and their backpacks return to the bus shelter. Several busses come and go before they find the Yellow Line.

Mia steps onto the bus first, then it's Jill's turn to climb aboard. As she grabs the rail and takes a second step, lifting her right foot from the street to join the left in the bus; her pack pulls her backward in a comical motion. Mia watches with humiliation as her friend holds onto the rail of the bus, completely extended; doing her best not to fall out. Her misstep with her backpack and the stairs lasts only a second, but was long enough for the driver and all the passengers to now become aware of her.

Jill recovers and does not fall out. She moves into the bus and turns to go down the aisle, looking forward to finding a refuge on the shuttle somewhere next to Mia. She feels the blunt impact of a young girl's head collide with her overstuffed burgundy pack. Jill pivots towards the victim to apologize, but as she does this, she hits the leg of the bus driver. Again she whirls around to say sorry to the driver, but realizes her actions are not working. She stands up, tries to wish herself narrow and sulks down the aisle of the bus. Carefully, she turns sideways before unloading the pack into the empty fiberglass seat in front of her.

A little shocked from attacking the locals, Jill grabs onto the seat in front of her and turns to Mia. "Mia, I knocked into that poor girl! I can't believe I just did that!" She lowers herself into the seat ashamed.

Mia gives Jill a nod. "You definitely did Jill. Let's just try to get to Zeeburg."

Mia slinks down into the hard seat.

The bus continues through the streets of Amsterdam. While sitting, Jill's mind works hard to process the fact that she's a guest in someone else's country and that she can't bludgeon locals with her luggage. Then she has an epiphany she knows she needs to share with Mia. "Look, Mia, I know you really want to blend in and resemble the locals. But, really . . . we are tourists. It will be easier if we start acting like tourists. I know I might seem odd, lost, and confused, . . . and I guess I am. What I'm trying to say is, it's okay."

Mia slides back up and tucks a loose strand of brown hair behind her ear. She gives her a silly look and whispers, "Jill we're in Amsterdam!"

Mia has a way of curing Jill's insecurities. As if, she has enough confidence for both of them. Her smile is contagious and together the two travelers beam with enthusiasm. They try to take in as many sights from the bus window as they might hope to remember.

Jill continues with her pep talk, now that she can see Mia is willing to hear reason. "We're going to be awkward and things are going to be challenging. Who cares? No one knows us here. Let's have fun, Mia!"

Mia puts her hand on top of Jill's, which is resting on the top of the seat, "The next stop is ours."

They both slide to the edge of their seats and wait, watching, wondering what the stop might look like. The driver slows down and engages the air brakes. The bus stops. Over a dated speaker his voice calls out with a flavorful accent, "Zeeburg."

The girls jump up and head to the side doors to hop out. This time Jill is determined not to harm anyone with her pack and carefully sidesteps her way to the exit.

The girls are left standing together on a worn stone sidewalk. They watch the bus drive away before identifying which way to go.

Deux

The bus moves further into the distance until it turns a corner and completely disappears. Mia and Jill realize this new environment will be less forgiving than the bus stops, shuttle stations, and airports.

"This way." Mia points, wanting to follow the sidewalk east.

Jill looks at the path designated by her friend. The sidewalk turns, then climbs over a waterway which seems to lead to an industrialized area. She can see factory smoke stacks releasing black clouds that hang just below the horizon. Jill considers her friend's suggestion, but can't accept the direction she believes they should go heads into a place with freight yards, factories, and small barges that transport cargo reside. Jill shakes her head. "It's definitely this way," she points west, opposite of her friend's choice.

Mia frowns.

"I mean, look, Mia, there is no way there's a campground over by those factories. Can you see a campground? It must be this way." Jill gestures to the houses lined along a quaint little street shaded by well-established trees.

The sun continues to lower and the two friends can feel the temperature drop just enough to make them retract their arms inward to conserve body heat. With arms tucked in and fingers hooked around the straps of her pack, Mia walks in the direction she believes to be correct. Knowing her friend all too well, Jill trails behind her in their original formation. Jill figures she can humor her friend who she can tell is in desperate need of a break from the moving about. As the two approach the place where the street lifts up, they can see a bridge that crosses some sort of canal. After several steps rising above the bridge their eyes focus on the destination they had been seeking. Directly below the bridge on a wide embankment and to the right, stretches a humble little field of grass. Two small buildings, and three camping tents stand out against the splash of green. Mia points with encouragement. "There it is!"

"We found it, Mia! I can't believe we did it!"

With a shift of their feet and a sway of their hips, they practically dance back down the sidewalk over to a small dirt path that winds downward to the campground.

The sun moves even lower until it's just a faint glimmer of what's been leftover from the day. The women stand outside of a small office with signs posted about in the windows and on the door. They both tousle their hair, readjust their packs, and mentally rehearse a greeting for the Amsterdam campground host. Jill notes the decorative hippie style "welcome" sign posted to the door. It has a dragon lounging on a bed of flowers. An attractive blonde close to Mia and Jill's age is inside. Mia's curiously impressed by the European front-desk attendant.

Jill steps forward and puts her hand on the desk. "Hi, we have reservations for the next two nights."

The svelte woman smiles warmly and takes a long observation of the weary travelers. The look made them squirm a little.

"Americans! Welcome to Zeeburg. You flew in today, yes? How was your flight?" She pauses unrushed, and waits for them to think of a simple but informative reply.

Mia answers, "Our flight was long. We're definitely ready for a shower, some food, and some rest."

Jill nods, backing up her friend's assessment.

"Of course," she pushes her golden locks of hair behind her ear and steps closer. "Your first night in Amsterdam and you're not planning on going out?" She smiles with empathy. She speaks while she prepares a few documents for the women to sign. She pulls down a small key from a tag board. "I think you're really going to like your stay here. You'll be in cabin number five. It's the last room at the end of the building. We have the bathroom and showers just out front in the long brown building. Next to this office there is a small café and a bar."

She nods at them with icy blue eyes then slides the paperwork over to Jill. Jill initials and signs, then picks up the key from the counter.

Together they turn to exit and call out, "Thank you."

Mia and Jill look around to assimilate to the new surroundings. What Jill thought was a canal is actually the river that the campground advertised in the brochure. Clouds are starting to build in the sky and a slight breeze hurries the girls along as they walk and look. Only a few more paces and they'll be able to roost down for a lazy night. Finally; shelter and comfort to rehabilitate them from the long and strenuous journey. The freshly cut grass slopes down to a fence, preventing travelers from ever reaching the water's edge, which seems to abruptly drop off. Across on the other side is another pasture of grass, but this one is full of cows instead of tents.

Beside the pasture of tents are two long buildings. One building is used for the bathrooms and showers. The other building is sectioned off into little sleeping cabins. This will be where Mia and Jill will sleep. At the end of the building is a cheerful looking courtyard with tables, pay phones, and a vending machine. Across from the buildings, framing the courtyard is the office where they checked in beside the café and bar.

An electric force seems to groan above them as lower clouds move a little quicker above heavy dark clouds. The sun is gone and a deep shade of night envelopes everything. The women can make out the land from the water, but that is all. The details will have to wait to be enjoyed tomorrow in the light of morning.

Mia works the key into the lock and the door springs open. A simple, but cramped room that has two sets of bunk beds invites them in. Both girls rush inward, flinging off their overstuffed packs. Mia raises her arms to stretch. Jill flops down on the closest bed. Together, without saying, they fathom this small achievement that required so much effort. The task is finished, and the reward manifests itself into four basic walls, and a roof. It's not glamorous or even very interesting, but for tonight: it's theirs and worth every square inch. Shoes are kicked off and layers are removed. The cabin room is decent, clean, and cozy. Mia sprawls out on the bed opposite of Jill. The fatigue of traveling has converted itself into an excitement from the newness of it all. Five full minutes of silence is shared.

Jill breaks the purity of the experience, "Showers or food? I need a beer from the bar! Can you imagine, Mia, new and different beers in Amsterdam!"

Mia, who's caught up in the dreaminess of the moment, responds with a sigh, "Let's shower and get cleaned up; put on fresh clothes; then go to the bar. Sound like a plan?"

"The perfect plan." Jill agrees.

.   .   .   .   .

Two showers later, the refreshed travelers are now radiant in clean clothes and heavily applied makeup. Mia is combing her damp hair back behind her ears with precision. Jill's working hard to clump her longer, wet hair into two buns. She fastens them just below her ears. Jill dives into her immense bag, she shuffles and rearranges until she pulls out a powder blue beanie which she places lovingly onto her damp head. She decides her beanie will do a good job representing her American style.

Mia has a nice European looking sweater and a pair of brown leather clogs.

"Are you ready to go find some food and drink, babe?"

Jill turns to Mia, "Hold on."

She rummages through the pile of dirty clothes and a travel towel before retrieving the flesh colored, silk-ish pocket thing that sprouts with zippers and cords. Jill hangs her traveler's pocket from her neck before she tucks the oddity down her shirt. It's safely hidden away from the notorious thieves who prey on innocent tourists staying in Amsterdam campgrounds.

"Okay, now I'm ready."

Mia swings open the door and a frigid gust of wind washes over the tight space. The women take a breath, then dash out the door. In haste they quietly navigate the dark path to the bar.

Mia opens the door. She holds it for her friend. The first thing they discover in the café are men relaxing in the far corner holding large mugs of beer. They go directly to the bar, pretending that they don't notice the obtrusive stares coming from the corner.

Jill and Mia hopelessly review the drink menu written in chalk on a tablet above the bartender's head.

"Hi." The bartender greets them in a brazen accent.

Standing in the front of the café; both women are victims of a sensorial assault and are unable to gear down the excitement of having walked into a bar in Amsterdam to order a beer for the very first time. Eyes big and gaping at the bartender who's sauntered over to them. He now has his elbows resting on the narrow counter, propping up his hands which hold his disinterested face. Somehow the demeanor of the bartender doesn't translate well, which amplifies Jill's nervousness and sharpens Mia's desire to order some dinner.

Mia answers with confidence, the confidence that makes Jill appreciate her all over again. "Hi. Can we get a couple beers. Are you still serving food?" Mia scans the bar for a menu or any hint of dinner.

"We have a small bar menu. It's listed up there," The bartender scratches his head, then points to a chalkboard in the corner.

Mia squints her eyes, trying to read the scribbles. The food is listed in English since they're at an international campground, but the prices are listed in Euros. Mia turns to Jill who's fishing out her traveler's pocket from under her clothing. She looks exaggerated and awkward as she keeps tugging and winding the cord until the pouch comes up and gets caught between her neck and chin. The pouch is pinned beneath the collar of her sweatshirt. Mia is momentarily distracted by this show, and waits with interest as her friend untangles the pocket pouch from her shirt, unzips it, and sifts through the modest contents, pulling out several Euros that she had purchased at a money exchange center at the airport. Mia shifts her weight to her other hip and faces the bartender again.

The bartender steps back and stretches himself a bit, extending over the bar.

The women examine their menu options.

Jill reads aloud. "Friet, I think that's fries, Pizza by the slice, a sausage on a roll, and cheese sandwiches." They both notice the cheese sandwiches are the most affordable for the bargain price of two Euro.

Mia steps forward and opens her wallet on the bar. Without making eye contact with the bartender she slowly gives him her order. "Can I have a cheese sandwich and a small glass of Heineken?"

"Sure," he replies. "That will be four Euro."

She hands him five for a tip.

It's Jill's turn. The bartender smiles at her, and she blushes as she fumbles with the Euro in one hand and the flesh colored travel pouch in the other. "Hi." Jill smiles, then raises her voice, pronouncing her order slowly. "Hi, can I have a cheese sandwich and a small glass of Heineken?"

"Yes." He answers systematically.

Jill passes him the five. He disappears to pour their beer. The bar is littered with Heineken signs. Signs are important, especially the ones the women can understand.

The two friends take their little beers and find a quiet corner with some comfy chairs. Mia takes a sip, then Jill.

"Well . . . what do you think?" Mia gives Jill a sly smile and tilts her glass again, which leaves the drink at the halfway mark.

"I think we're going to have a really good time. We ordered our first food and drink in Europe; didn't go so bad! Here's to us! What should we do tomorrow?"

Mia sets the glass down, staring at it as she considers the question, "You know Jill, I don't even think it matters. Let's just grab our wallets and wander around Amsterdam."

"I'm so excited, I can't even sleep now. I'm going to need a lot more of these mini beers before I'll be able to crash tonight. Especially after that flight," Jill exasperates, using her index finger to play with the condensation on her glass.

Mia raises her glass, "Here's to conquering our international flight."

Jill clinks her glass with Mia's, "To our flight." The Mini-beers are tipped back and before the empty glasses are set down, two mini plates with two mini cheese sandwiches are set on the side table, between the two comfy chairs.

"Here are you're sandwiches. Would you like another beer?" The bartender stands sweetly and exchanges a nod with the thirsty girls. "I'll be back then, sweethearts."

Both women giggle at his endearment.

"I'll get this round," Jill offers, catching her companion before she has time to pull out her wallet.

"Oh, no, you're going to pull that weird thing out of your sweatshirt again!" She starts to laugh. "I think I'll need a few more drinks before I can handle watching you fight with your neck pocket again! Thanks for the drink. Maybe we should go shopping for a new purse for you tomorrow. Wouldn't it be sweet to have a purse from Amsterdam?"

Jill shakes her head, then smiles. "You're just jealous!"

"Of your pocket thing? Umm, I have pockets built into my clothes like normal people."

Jill retorts, "You'll thank me after you get pick-pocketed, and have no identification or money in a foreign land, and I'll be there to bail you out. Insurance, baby!" She winks at Mia who can't help but laugh.

Two beers replace two empty glasses, and sips of a hoppy concoction paired with nibbles of cheese sandwiches seem to fully bring the girl's into their moment. Jill and Mia in a bar in Amsterdam.

"Mia, is it bad that we didn't really make a solid itinerary? Should we have scheduled or planned to do more things?"

"Hmmm, I don't know yet, Jill. I think we'll be okay. There's a botanical garden I want to visit, so we can plan on doing that."

"I definitely insist that we go see the Louvre in Paris!"

Mia smiles. "We will."

All of the sudden the women are yanked out of their little peaceful bubble by four very handsome, mysterious strangers.

"Hello girls," a tall red haired twenty-four year old says in a burly Irish accent.

Jill and Mia have no time to organize themselves or process the intrusion of the newly found abundance of handsomeness.

Surrounded, these odds are looking more than good. Two of the gentleman have reddish hair, while the other two have dark brown. Three of the men have striking green eyes, while one has deep brown eyes.

Then, one more. "Do you mind if I squeeze in?" An American man in his twenties appears, going directly to Mia. He's aggressive and claims a place sitting right beside her in the cozy chair which could probably fit two small people or one large person. Mia is small, and the American guy is large, so things become even cozier. Everyone has a drink in hand and the night starts to feel like a real occasion.

Mia takes charge, which works, since she seems to have the majority of the attention from the testosterone-charged group. "So, what are your names? Where are you from?"

They start to laugh, which is good, and the girls can tell these very confident, good-looking men are already a little buzzed. This relaxes them and gives both women permission to act less formal and a little more playful. It also entices them to try to catch up.

Counter clockwise they each introduce themselves. "I'm Mickey, from Ireland, and I'm a Virgo," he says, making his voice low and flirtatious.

"I'm Sean from Ireland, and I'm a Leo," he gives Jill a spirited nod.

"I'm Paul from Ireland, and I'm a Pisces."

I'm Thomas from Ireland, and I don't know what the hell I am, maybe a crab or bull man or something."

Sean adds; "That's right, ladies, we call him the bull man, and he's no joke." He winks at Mia and Jill, who seem a little confused, but really happy.

In a louder voice, wanting attention, the American speaks. "I'm Addison and I'm from Wisconsin." Addison's arrogance drowns out the sweetness and foolishness offered by the Irish.

Jill's happy to cross paths with another American and hopes she can pick his brain about what to do and see on her own adventure. "Addison, are you traveling alone?"

He scoots himself a bit further away from Mia so they aren't making contact. "Sort of. I had a girl who I was traveling with, but she stayed back in Spain to live on the beach for a while. We've been beach bumming down there for almost a month, and I wasn't that into it. I like it here in Amsterdam." He runs his hand over the top of his hair, smooth and cool.

Jill studies the globalized young American. He's tan and his brown hair is faded from sun. He has big brown eyes and a great smile. He's in a sweatshirt similar to her own. She decides she's glad to be sitting in a group that includes him.

Thomas takes the conversation back. "Come on, girls. You didn't just fly all the way from America to sit and visit with an American, did you?"

Jill finishes mini beer number two, then answers faithfully, "Nope, I've never met a real Irish person before. I mean, my family has an Irish origin, and I know a little bit about the culture, but I had no idea how much I would love your accent!"

"Well, Jill, there's a lot you'll love about us Irish men. Toast it up lads!" Everyone lifts their beer in praise of themselves. "Irish men!"

Jill and Mia are delighted at the jovial, warm personalities that surround them.

For the rest of the evening, the five men compete for attention and a chance to entertain both women. Cordial and bright, the conversation never seems to dull. The five campers have been spending a good amount of time at the campground and are thrilled to welcome two young twenty-somethings, fresh from America, to fill the void of the evening. Despite the flirting, they make more of a sweet impression. Even though they'd dial up the sleaze, it's more in a joking way than in a sleazebag style.

. . . . .

"Last call," The stoic bartender shouts over to the enthusiastic group, who are now clustered around the pool table. They're enjoying their second round of pool, Mia's taken the red headed team, and Jill is thrilled to be on Sean and Mickey's team.

"We should go to bed, Jill," Mia suggests, assessing that the evening could use some intervention before too much fun brings regret their way.

Jill nods at Mia, but is more than distracted by one Irish man in particular. He has a clingy grey sweater that she thinks looks amazing against his green eyes and buzzed dark hair.

"Huh?", she responds, trying to watch him without being noticed. He seems to be talking more to Mia, but Jill doesn't care. She's just thrilled to get to watch him, and to be in a group with such a fascinating stranger. His name is Mickey, like the malt liquor back home she used to love in high school.

"We should go to bed now."

"Oh, yeah, let's go to bed." Jill's happy to comply with Mia, who seems to be a little more skilled at managing the new group of almost-friends.

"Goodnight, boys. We're off to bed. It's been a good one." Mia grabs Jill's hand and they head for the exit. Jill's happy for her friend, and for her new friends, and for Amsterdam, and campgrounds, and a trip that's gotten off to a great start.

Lights are switched off and pool cues are laid to rest across the table. The men collect in an orderly mass and head for the exit behind the women. Mia pushes the door to step out, but a gust of wind pushes it back. She has to use both hands and her weight to push it open again. A blast of cold night air drifts into the bar. The entire group, who have been the only patrons for the entire night, stagger out into the wet storm. Without discussing the next plan of action, the entire group bolts across the courtyard and rushes into the bathrooms; girls on one side, boys on the other.

Jill and Mia curve around a floating privacy wall. They stop to embrace the warmth and dryness of the brightly lit bathroom. After selecting a stall and washing their hands and face, they're finally ready for bed.

"Hey, Mia, its crazy windy and cold out there. What do think about offering to let those guys stay in the cabin with us tonight? We have two extra beds, and all the space on the floor for their sleeping bags. I hate to think of them trying to sleep and stay warm in a tent tonight."

Mia smiles. "I think it's a good idea, too. They're really nice. I have a thing for redheads. Paul is so hot."

The girls laugh and charge out of the bathroom hoping to run into the men one more time to invite them back. Jill sees Addison and Sean across the dark courtyard in front of a vending machine.

"Hey, boys!" Jill waves. They walk over to seek shelter next to the women who are hugging themselves to retain all the body heat they can manage below the slim awning of the restroom.

"Hey, ladies. What's up?" Addison winks at Mia.

Jill turns to Sean, "We were talking . . . and it's so windy and rainy tonight . . . do you guys want to get your sleeping bags and stay in the cabin room with us? It's small, but we can all squeeze in." She blushes as if she's just confessed a terrible secret.

"Oh, my God, girls, that would be lovely. You're saints. I'll go grab my things right now," Sean proclaims with gratitude.

"Cool, and make sure to let the others know they should come too. Okay?" Mia gently suggests, hoping to see her red head one more time this evening.

"Sure. Thanks, Mia. Thanks, Jill." Sean smiles. He and Addison walk away, vanishing into the dark meadow.

Arm in arm, the girls begin the quick walk back to their cabin. Mia thinking about Paul with a dreamy and buzzed smile on her face, and Jill thinking about Mickey, not even daring to imagine she could actually have an official crush on him. Once inside the anticipation starts to build.

They lock eyes and roar with laughter.

"Is this okay? Can we do this? Pick up five guys in a bar and bring them back with us?" Jill asks, checking in with her friend's moral code.

"Well, you make it sounds worse than it is, Jill. I mean, it's nasty out there. Those guys would do the same thing for us if we were in their position."

Jill nods, realizing the beer and late hour of the night is starting to weigh on her. "Hmmm, well should we share a bunk bed and give them the other?"

"Sounds good. I'll take the top bunk." Mia grabs her things which are currently spread across one bed. She tosses them up to her new little nest.

"Mia, this is crazy. This is weird. We just got here and now we're having a slumber party with Irish boys. It's too good, Mia. We are so badass."

Mia giggles. "I know."

Then a single knock on the door. Jill reaches her arm out and pulls open the door. In pours five wet men with pillows and sleeping bags in hand.

"Hello girls. Thanks for letting us stay here tonight." Paul says with warmth and sweetness in an accent that makes both girls melt.

The rest of the men echo in agreement. "Yes, thank you."

"Oh, please, you'd do the same for us." Mia responds and gives Paul a lingering smile before giving the others smiles.

"It's appreciated, lass. If we weren't here tonight, I'd have to be cuddling up to Mickey there to stay warm. That can lead to an awkward feeling the next day you know." Sean winks at Jill.

"Yes, it's not natural to cuddle you're mucker." Mickey adds.

The red heads grab the bunk bed, the two brunettes and the American find just enough space to lay out their bags on the floor. The women have to stay in their spots on their bunks in order for everyone to fit. Soon the light flips off and seven strangers lie a little drunk. The only sound is of a howling wind beating against the thin paneled walls of the cabin.

Everyone wants to have the same conversation. The conversation is called: The United States meets Ireland. The Irish want to formally introduce the Americans to the finer points of their very special gem of a country. The Americans want to brag about how the United States is the most amazing place ever. In the end the Irish are more passionate about teaching the Americans about Ireland, than listening to the Americans arrogance about their own country. This could be because many people have a pretty broad understanding of the United States, but it also could be that the Irish could tell Addison, Mia, and Jill knew very little about how fantastic Ireland is. Where the Americans sound smug and boastful, the Irish appear interesting and passionate when sharing information about their home. Somehow, at one point the conversation turns to singing, and the singing is heartfelt and serious as one drunken red-headed Irishman begins to belt out "Oh Danny Boy". After giggles and laughter, and the sharing of other Irish ballads everyone finally passes out.

Morning comes quickly. Everyone wakes. Jill studies the room. Amazingly enough, all seven drunk people had enough self-control that nothing funny took place last night.

Jill thinks to herself; "These guys are real gentleman. They are so genuine and told stories, and sung songs, and are right here on the floor. "Did I actually fall asleep last night listening to someone singing Oh Danny Boy?" Jill has a mental chuckle while stalling to fully awaken. Jill can feel her crush on not just Mickey but the whole group of these Irish travelers grow, and it feels fun and light. She easily likes every single person in the cabin and is happy for this.

Mia hangs her head down, half falling onto Jill's bunk. "Good morning. Rise and shine, my carrot muffin."

Jill grins at Mia, and neither of them can contain their excitement to experience their first morning in Europe.

"It's going to be a good day, my friend," Jill says to Mia. They have a moment. Mia's trying to communicate something with her eyes. Jill has no freaking idea what she's trying to say. She can't even guess. The men are rising too. They retrieve their belongings into their arms, holding them against their bodies, looking tired from the long night. "Well, Mia, we'll get going now. I really need to go take a shower." Sean states, his green eyes sparkling. He has the best eyes out of all the men.

Then Paul speaks, "What are you two up to today? Are you going to see any sights?"

Jill answers. "I think today we might just wander the city, shop, checkout the café's, maybe a museum."

"You might like the flea market then," Paul suggests, as he rubs the sleep from his eyes. "We're going to go clean up and put our stuff away. We can meet you in the courtyard in an hour if you'd like us to show you some spots."

Jill looks at Mia. They don't answer, still considering the proposition.

"It's the least we can do, since you both were so nice to let us sleep inside, away from the storm." Mickey adds, while stretching his arms and pushing out his chest.

The girls look at one another one more time. "Do you want to Mia?"

She answers Jill, "The flea market sounds pretty cool."

"It was pretty hard figuring out the bus systems and city blocks yesterday. It would be a lot better if we had a tour guide or two." Jill leans in and whispers in Mia's ear,"Hot tour guides."

Mia grins.

She turns to the Irishmen. "Yes, we would really like that. If you're not busy today!"

Paul runs his hand through his wavy ginger hair, "Consider it a date."

The combination of the hand through the red hair, and the word date, requires Mia to lock her knees, otherwise she might just fall over.

The men are gone, and the cabin is once again occupied by two American women. The room looks as if they were never there, which makes Jill feel a little sad. There's a great mutual energy that buzzes about the group. They synergize in an unusual way. Everything's so comfortable and good. The room feels so empty immediately after the men leave. The women are confronted with so many different thoughts racing through their jet-lagged brains. Thoughts regarding traveling, bus routes, Irish men, cabins, breakfast, hangovers, showers, what to wear, and other random decisions that require definitive action.

"So, Miss Jill, we better go grab some showers so we can get into some fresh clothes for today. Amsterdam baby!"

During their short-ten minute showers, Jill and Mia chat. Not about Europe or culture, but of course what seems to be the universal Achilles heel of most women . . . they chat about men.

"Paul is a dream boat." Mia declares, as she tries to vigorously towel dry her hair before wrapping it up turban style.

Jill nods and thinks about Mickey again, but decides to keep the crush to herself. She's sure she has no chance with him and doesn't see the point in sharing the hopeless attraction with her friend. She pushes the thought from her mind, and instead, focuses on the fun of the day. Jill takes her towel and tries her best to turn it into a neat tight turban like Mia's. It twists, then relaxes before falling down in front of her face. Jill flops it back up and holds it in place with her hand.

While the women studiously apply mascara and lip gloss, Mia turns to Jill with a mischievous smile. Jill gives her friend her immediate attention.

"Yeah . . . so last night, Jill, I hate to tell you this, but you were farting in your sleep." She smiles with her eyes and her mouth, but not in a mean way. The kind of smile that shows honest, supportive friendship.

Jill puts her hand to her mouth and gasps, "Oh, my god! I was?" Thoughts pour into Jill's mind excessively. She imagines the tiny little room in the dark, with the wall-to-wall, floor-to-ceiling Irish men; she thinks of the noises and how they would have sounded. She thinks "Was Mia telling the truth? Of course, she is; no way is she making that up."

"Oh, God, I'm so embarrassed! What should I do?" Jill panics, still covering her mouth with her hand.

"Yeah, you passed out pretty quickly, and you must have just been really tired and relaxed." Mia tries to help by offering an explanation.

"I mean; oh, no, I think I must have been holding in all my gas over that really long plane ride. As soon as I fell asleep my body probably needed to deal with some issues. This is so horrible. Worst case scenario, Mia. Worst case scenario!" The fact that this traumatic situation's occurred is too horrible to deal with; Jill can't even cry. She's devastated.

Mia laughs. "It's really not that bad." She has a great big smile on her face thinking of the humorous way her friend treads through the world. "Hey, you know . . . after I fell asleep, I was probably farting, too."

This thought oddly brings Jill comfort. "Really?"

Mia can see the complete look of horror consuming her friend's expression. "Yeah, I'm sure I was. But, I still told the guys it was you." Mia fake punches her friend in the side and they both start to laugh.

Mia's attempts to comfort helps. Jill accepts she has no other choice. She would have to follow her friends lead through this situation. There is no other solution. She can't change the past. Mia grins. "Don't worry about it Jill. They were probably drunk and won't remember."

"Do you think some of them slept through it, and maybe they didn't hear?" Jill spoke with such deep hope, fishing for an idea or belief that might undo the offense she's been deemed guilty of.

"Oh, yeah, I'm sure some of them were asleep."

Jill inspects Mia's face, trying to decide if her friend is simply humoring her, or if some of the Irishmen really could have passed out. Jill can't read Mia. She shakes her head and sighs.

"Come on, let's plan our day. Anything you want to do, Jill."

"I just want to hide in the cabin, or we could just leave for Paris now!"

"You're okay, Jill. Besides, who cares about those guys and what they think? We'll never see them again after we leave."

Jill nods her head again and continues to apply make-up. More and more makeup, to cover up and hide behind. By the time she's done, her nervousness is plastered all over her face. Thick black eyeliner, freakishly shiny glossed lips, and caked on concealer, so thick you can carve initials into her face.

Fresh and ready for the day, Jill follows Mia's lead out the door of the cabin to approach the picnic tables in the courtyard where their Irish escorts are waiting. Jill studies them from this distance and tries to prepare to seem confident in the light of day. They look as charming and exotic as they had last night. Irishmen, so European looking, fitted jackets with the collars flipped up, modest brown leather shoes, dark washed jeans, defined bone structure in their cheeks, and Jill's favorite; those earth toned wool sweaters that make them look like they've been casting fishing nets out on a remote and windy sea, in a place distant and far away from the familiar sights of California. Jill could stare at the green-eyed, sweater-wearing men all day long. The best part is they seem to enjoy being stared at. They're comfortable with visiting, and casual stories, and fun. They're warm and sweet, and seem to value the American's company.

With each step, Jill does her best to push the thought from her mind. But it just keeps insisting. She thinks: "They heard me fart. They heard me fart. Was I loud? They heard me fart." She walks directly behind her friend, trying to hide and be so small. Perhaps they would dismiss her, or forget about her existence completely.

As they arrive to join the group of handsome Irishmen, Mia saves Jill. Mia starts to talk, and not to the men, but to her friend. "Our first whole day in Amsterdam, Jill! We are going to have so much fun."

"Would you girls like to go to the market first? They have street vendors, good food, and crappy stuff to buy." Paul greets them with anticipation and a smile.

Mia looks at Jill. "Sound good, Jill?"

Jill nods her head in compliance.

Sean and Mickey are sitting on top of the picnic table. They slide off and turn to the women. "We're going to do some things today, but we hope we'll see you later."

They give each girl a heavy wink and a finger point, before turning to leave. Jill and Mia blush, then take the open spot on the table where the men were sitting. Mia turns to Paul. "I saw a sign for a botanical garden. Have you been there?"

Thomas lifts his eyes to try to remember a garden. "Nope, haven't been there. But, if you'd like to go . . . we can go there today."

Addison scoots closer to Mia. "You like gardens, too. I think they're amazing." Mia arches her eyebrow at the transparency of Addison's fake interest in horticulture.

"That's what I study in school. I love plants and trees." Mia replies coolly, waiting for the reaction from the men.

"Plants and trees, huh? That's interesting, Mia. If we go, can you teach me some things about horticulture?" Paul asks.

Mia rolls her shoulders back and straightens her lean posture. "I would love to."

Jill quietly observes the complex day that unfolds before her. She notes to herself; "Addison likes Mia. Paul likes Mia. Mia likes Paul." Then Jill looks over at Thomas. It seems he's just hanging out, not trying to compete with the other two. Then Jill adds: "no one likes me, the sleep-farting girl." Fortunately, everyone seems happy and inclusive with Jill, despite her nighttime condition. She thinks about Mia's words of comfort. "Perhaps Mia was right, it's not a big deal. No one cares."

And so, the happy group of travelers embark on their journey, exploring the streets of Amsterdam.

Trois

One stroll through the street market, one trip through the botanical gardens where they view plants and trees from California on display, and their first whole day in Amsterdam passes effortlessly. For the bulk of the afternoon Jill finds herself left to the side, while Thomas, Paul, and Addison compete for Mia's affection. Paul isn't as aggressive, and it's hard to tell if he even feels an attraction to Mia. Thomas is carried away with the challenge and initiates several deep conversations with Mia about plants and the Golden State. Jill can see immediately that Thomas's connection to horticulture and California is purely fake. She only hopes Mia is picking up on his false enthusiasm.

.   .   .   .   .

The bright-eyed group stands in front of an empty park. They're spending time in a green belt that meanders through the old city. It shines an emerald hue, giving a fresh look to the weathered stone roads and aged bricks of the buildings. The men sit on a little wooden bench. Mia and Jill stand. Happy to stretch their legs after the long flight the yesterday.

"Did we really just spend the day looking at trees from back home?" Jill says. Teasing her friend in amusement.

"Oh, come on. Those guys have never seen a Sequoia before in their entire life. How cool is that? That native Californians got to show them their first Sequoia!" Mia answers. She's thrill continues to stay with her from having toured some of her favorite trees and shrubs.

Jill nods with complacency. It was cool to show them. She has to admit, Mia's right. It was fascinating to watch her play tour guide for the group while they walked among the flowers. Mia's so excited and passionate when she speaks about plants, pointing out unique characteristics, or what she specifically likes best about them. She opened minds this afternoon, and helped them to rethink objects they may have taken for granted. It was earthy and wholesome, but it just wasn't Amsterdam enough. Jill needs to see more of the region's culture. She feels greed and conviction as she looks with her eyes, wanting to know what this place. She ponders the function of Amsterdam.

Jill turns to Mia. "Let's go get some groceries from that market across the street. We can get sandwich stuff for dinner and share it with the guys."

Mia turns to her competitive ginger-kissed men. "You guys can go ahead and take this bus back. Jill and I will catch the next one. We want to try to ride the bus system on our own, without your help."

The men are happy to fulfill the object of their affections wish and leave the women to their shopping.

"I just need some time with you, Jill. Addison is really starting to annoy me." Mia sighs.

"Really? You didn't seem to mind Addison earlier when he paid for our coffee. I noticed you and Thomas had a moment in that rose garden!"

Mia shakes her head, "He's okay. I think I want to know Paul better. It's just hard with Thomas and Addison always stepping in. I do kind of like Thomas, too." She turns to gaze at a shade tree. She withdraws; lost in conflict. She looks the way a cat does after catching a mouse.

"Poor Lass! Too many men fancy her!" Jill teases in a bad attempt at an Irish accent.

Mia's caught with nothing to say. Jill has a point.

"I'm glad you sent them away. It's been distracting having them around all day. Now, we can just hang out." Jill reassures her friend's impulsive decision.

Mia takes a longer look at the store, before they cross the street to experience the Dutch curiosity. Everything is new and different; even visiting a grocery store and purchasing food feels like a challenging adventure. Inside the store, the women are occupied with so many different types of foods. The packaging isn't familiar and the words are unrecognizable. Clueless, doing their best to keep a muse in mind, they end up moving to the back of the store.

"There!" Mia points to baskets full of fresh baked bread in paper sleeves.

They pick out four baguettes that are still warm from the oven. Next they locate the cheese. They pick out something cream-colored. They find themselves standing in front of a case of deli meat. The meat in the Dutch case is very different looking. There are many types of cured and sliced sandwich meats, but they don't look the same as they would in the United States. They aren't finding anything that looks like ham or turkey. Eventually they manage to find a package that resembles salami of some sort.

"The mystery meats look intense. Should we just stick to the salami?" Jill's hungry, she's ready to get what they need and locate a bus back to the campground to hang out, and eat.

"Okay, do we need condiments?"

The two women scan the store and feel unsure of where the condiments might be, or what they might look like. Giving up on condiments, they grab a few tomatoes and a package of sprouts for the sandwiches. Surrendering to hunger, they grab a few bunches of green grapes and head up to the counter to purchase their dinner.

.   .   .   .   .

Soon the American women navigate their way back to the campground, each with a nice brown bag stuffed with food. Unsatisfied with what they ended up purchasing, they got over the lack of tasty dinner by the excitement of a meal with their new interesting friends. The entire way back; Mia explores the options of her crush on Paul, then of her interest in Thomas, the whole time vocalizing her disinterest in Addison, who can't take a hint. Jill thinks Addison is nice, but his pursuit of her friend has definitely become obnoxious, especially by the end of the day. The storm dissipated over the course of the morning and an open sky shows blue above a lush meadow sprinkled with tents. The courtyard tables are perfect for a few beers and some dry sandwiches on soft fresh bread.

The sun drops lower into the cityscape, dipping down to hide below the skyline of the city. All the food is finally devoured, nibble after nibble, until all that remains are a few empty cans of beer and an empty paper bag on the picnic table. Lighter sweaters and shirts are now layered beneath heavier jackets, and, for Jill, a sweatshirt. Mickey and Sean have joined the group and have with them a round of Heineken (which seems to be the only beverage anyone drinks at the campground).

Mia turns to Jill. "Jill, we need to register for the cabin tonight."

Jill stands up to reorganize herself. "I completely forgot!"

The two girls turn their direction to the cabin to retrieve their wallets when Addison interrupts. "You two don't need to pay for another night. If you want, you can stay in our tents and save some money."

The American women stop, catch one another's eyes and share a feeling. "Do you want too?" Mia asks, giving Jill a yes-look with her eyes.

Jill visualizes the evening, jammed in a tent with the men. They spent the entire evening last night, all day today, and now this evening they want to share sleeping quarters again? It feels a little aggressive and odd, but the men are intoxicating with their accents and rugged, travelled appearance.

She wonders if it's an innocent invitation, or if they have something more intentional in mind. She remembers the farting incident the night before, and hangs her head sadly. She lifts her worried face to address her ally. "Yes, let's do it. We'll save forty dollars!"

Paul chimes in. "It would make us happy to return the favor to you. You've been so great, letting us stay in the cabin last night, and for the sandwiches."

An image of hippie communal living pops into Jill's head as she considers the redistribution of sleeping quarters, sandwiches, and the generous sharing of beer that seems to miraculously appear on the picnic table.

Mia and Jill turn in the opposite direction and head to the campground office to unregister before it closes for the night. They return the key and wave to the foreign beauty at the front desk.

"Thank you." Jill boasts throwing her voice so it bounces against the far wall in the small office. This causes the attractive woman to flinch.

Mia herds her friend out the door. In a whisper she tries to reason with Jill, "You kind of shouted in there. You don't have to talk loud. Everyone speaks English around here. Besides, just saying it louder doesn't mean she'll understand it better."

Jill blushes, she didn't even realize she was yelling. She just wanted to communicate and figured she was being thoughtful in the process. She spent so much time planning for the potential to be robbed or harmed, she never considered that she would be the one sending out nasty vibes and injuring young girls on buses. Humbled, Jill walks cautiously behind her friend.

The women retrieve their backpacks and set them on the table behind the picnic table where everyone sits. Addison pounces before the women even have a chance to coordinate a sleeping arrangement.

"Do you see the tent way out in the corner of the field? That's mine. I'm all alone and have plenty of room to store your packs. Don't worry, ladies, I'll carry them over for you." Addison walks over to the backpacks, making a show of his masculine good intentions, raising each pack over one shoulder. He takes his time, showboating past all the drinkers at the table. Mia frowns as she watches her backpack moving away in the night, far from the blue tent that belongs to Paul. She shutters at the thought of a long cold night in between the conceited American and her dear friend's bad gas. The thought causes her to open a second beer.

The cool of the night and the long day together brings a lull in the conversation. Everyone listens intently to an argument between Sean and Mickey who are discussing the best way to start a campfire. Waterproof matches, the friction of sticks, magnification and other clever ingenuities are brainstormed. Jill finishes her third beer and decides she's had enough of the fire talk.

"I want to see the river." She looks out at the black ribbon of space that shows negative light under the cloak of a young evening. The stars are out tonight and she can't understand why the water fails to reflect them.

"You want to see the river, lass?" Sean jumps up from his spot on the tabletop.

"Yes! Why is there a fence all the way around it?" Jill asks.

"I know how to get down to it. I know where the fence ends," Sean flirts. He's obviously had the most beer. He's loud and lively, and equally ready to mix in some fun, just like Jill.

Jill shakes her head with doubt. "I don't want to go too far. I mean the river's right there. I was just saying it would be fun to get to actually go up and see the water." She feels happy. "I've never seen an Amsterdam river!" The thought of meeting a brand new river pulls her back into moment. She remembers these are her moments, and she came to capture them.

"Don't worry, angel. It's not far at all. Just up the bridge," Sean promises.

The other men stand up, starting to zip and button coats.

"Yeah, let's go for a walk then," adds Paul, who seems inspired by the miniature trip out of the campground. Jill watches Mia as she catches a sultry glimpse of Paul running his hand through the red hair. Jill wonders how he knows to do that.

"Alright then, let's go, you funny hobos!" Mickey hollers, joining in the ranks beside Sean.

"Wait! I have to do something!" Jill says, before leaving the group. With a skip in her step, she heads out into the dark field towards Addison's tent. She passes him on the way. "We're going to the river! I have to get something!"

The men turn their attention to Mia while they wait for Jill. Mia appreciates the attention and deduces that her crazy friend is probably going to collect her cameras to try to get some pictures in the dark of a dark body of water. It doesn't matter, she likes the odd way her friend perceives life. She imagines she'll enjoy seeing the end result of the photos.

Soon, all seven campers, resembling six dwarves following Mia -their Snow White, walk up and over a bridge, down the other side, until they find an open space below. Everyone walks and spreads out under the embankment. The graffiti under the bridge is colorful and impressive. It seems less hostile than the gang graffiti Jill is used to back home. Everyone grows quiet, enjoying the images and words painted on the stone walls of the bridge. They stare into the deep murky water.

"Perfect!" squeals Jill.

At some point, she gets over herself. It was shortly after Mia corrected her for speaking too loud in the registration office. She doesn't care, and decides that this is her vacation, her night, and she's going to enjoy it, her way. In other words, she's not concerned with the sexy Irish men or her very good and loyal companion. This is her own fun, and she's orchestrating the whole group activity. They're all there; together under a sketchy bridge late at night because of her, and everyone seems amused by her novel idea. This makes her feel entirely better.

Mia watches with interest, always anticipating a good show when it comes to Jill. In classic "Jill" form, she watches her friend double over and start to pull a bunched up object from beneath her sweatshirt.

"Ah, hah!" Jill shouts with joy.

She now has everyone's full attention. Mia laughs when she realizes Jill didn't go to fetch a camera. There she is, holding out her over-stretched jeans with the holes in them, waving them like a victory flag.

"This is it, Mia! I finally get to realize my dream!"

Jill walks over to the river's edge in a dramatic stride. She thinks for a second, then bunches the pants up into a jumbled ball. With all her might and her junior high basketball throw, she hucks the holey pair of jeans into the river. With a splash, she stops to watch in silence. Everyone else is at a loss for words as they witness the single act of self-expression, wishing to make sense of it.

Mickey is standing just a few feet up river from Jill. She can't see him, but he has the biggest inspired smile for her. With seven pairs of eyes refusing to take their gaze off the crumpled object, they watch in astonishment. First the ball of pants is tossed up and down on a swift current upriver. Then like a lotus blossom, it starts to expand and float on the surface, until it reclaims it's perfect and triumphant jean structure. A bloated, floating pair of pants sails past the group. They step forward, trying to get a last look before it disappears into the night while the forces of water begin to pull it under. Paul salutes the pants as they pass by.

Jill is done. She didn't say anything or try to do anything. Throwing away her old pants is enough. It's been her goal and she owns it. The jean sacrifice marks a rite of passage, a journey out into the world. It doesn't matter what it might seem like to the camping guys. She knows Mia understands and recognizes the pants that fit too tight.

"Okay, are we ready to go get beer?" Sean recruits. He puts his arm tenderly around Jill to walk her back to the bridge stairwell.

"I was ready twenty minutes ago you fucking chancers!" Thomas laughs, rubbing his hands together for warmth. "Come on, Mia, let's get back to the Heineken." He offers her his arm. She locks on. Every one falls in line, and the buzzed procession marches straight to the bar.

Just like the night before, the bar is empty, except for Addison, Jill and Mia and their Irish men. With the late hours of the evening approaching, the tension in the bar seems to collect among the intimate crowd. Angst and motive are rising closer to the surface. The competition for Mia's affection grows fierce and even Thomas seems to be divulging in the affair. Mia counters these flirtations by focusing her attention to Sean and Mickey who aren't hopelessly trying to romance the attractive American woman. This is more comfortable for both Mia and Jill, because Sean and Mickey are hilarious.

Jill's laughing and enjoying a lively conversation with Sean. "So how long have you and Mickey been traveling together?"

"Well, my dear, we've been here at Zeeburg for almost two months, but we've been moving around and visiting some other places as well. Oh, let's see . . . I think we've been away from Ireland for about five months."

"Five months!" Jill imagines being away from home, not having a home, just living as a young nomad for half a year.

"Yeah, I think we're going to head back next month. We're running low on money and we both have things to do back home," Sean explains, looking a bit mysterious.

Mia and Jill lean in with intrigue, "So, you guys just travel? You do this every day? You just hang out and drink and do nothing all day long? You just go see stuff and drink beer?" Jill asks bluntly.

"Yeah. Why not?" Mickey replies. "Isn't that why you two came here? To drink beer and look at stuff."

Jill and Mia are quiet, trying to gain perspective on this question.

Mia answers with a smile. "Yes, we're definitely here to travel and see things, have experiences, and I guess we do enjoy beer."

"You act like the whole idea of traveling and experiencing the world is brand new to you. In our culture young people are encouraged to go out and connect with other regions and ideas. It makes one more . . . hmmm . . . well-rounded," Mickey slurs his dry insight, before taking another sip.

Mia and Jill who have had the biggest ego boosts of their lives since they embarked on their trip, now feel small, maybe even a little bit ignorant. Mia's completely affected by the altruistic way Europe seems to flow and connect. This is a different type of value system, one that she' never considered before. This coming together, and meeting of the minds between the United States and Ireland over drinks with no specific purpose is illuminating, and exactly the type of experience the women have hoped to gain.

"So you went shopping, enjoyed some Dutch coffee and you saw some plants today. What else did you want to see in Amsterdam my darlings?" Sean slides closer to the two women. He slips his arm with debonair around Mia. Mia likes his warm teddy bear arm and rests into it some.

Mia's eyes glimmer, and her voice drops in pitch with her answer. "I want to see the café's."

Jill leans in and adds with sinister fun, "Have you seen the red light district? I want to check it out!"

"What? You haven't been to smoke at the café's yet?" Then he turns and winks at Jill. "We are going to take you to the Red Light District tomorrow, peaches."

Jill realizes they spent the day with the wrong Irishmen. Sean and Mickey are more scrupulous, they seem to have a passionate theory about how to live life. Sean leans over and grabs Jill's chair. He pulls it closer to Mia and himself, then puts his free arm around her. The girls settle into his bullish hug as he gives every other guy in the bar a fiery grin.

"It's a date then!" Shouts, Mia, as she slips away from Sean and peels off her cardigan. "Are you guys going to come with us tomorrow night?" She turns her gaze towards Thomas and waits for his answer. Jill notices that her friend's attention has slightly shifted from Paul to Thomas. Jill scoots her chair a few inches away from Sean.

"If you want us to come Mia, we would love to be your chaperones for the Red Light District. It's our honor," Thomas replies, in the cadence of his accent, which has a way of hypnotizing the American females.

Jill stands up. She's become bored with the uneventful way the day's progressed. She honestly just can't watch any more playful flirting between her friend and these men. Her evening is going nowhere, and what she really wants to do, more than touring the notorious Red Light District, is to go to Paris. She's dying to get on the train and move on, to whatever is waiting for her in quite possibly one of the most romantic cities in the world. She wants to see Notre Dame and the Louvre. She wants to shop and eat croissants.

"Where are you headed, sweetheart?" Sean's getting drunk, he's becoming more familiar.

Jill gives him a sincere look and confesses, "I'm so tired. I think I have jet lag. I'm just going to bed now."

"Oh, little lamb, stay up a bit longer with us. I promise to make it worth it, if you do." He offers, doing his best to keep the group together a little longer. He flips the collar of his jacket up and gives Jill a ravenous stare that causes her to squirm.

Addison jumps in to intervene. "You can stay in my tent, Jill. It's nice and quiet, tucked in the corner. We'll be down to join you really soon." He gives Mia a clever nod.

Jill really likes Addison, and he's been such a comrade. Addison has been the only American they've crossed paths with so far, and she's grateful for him. He's worldly and classy. Jill decides that if she were Mia, she would prefer to have a romance with Addison over the eccentric, but oh, so, irresistible Irish men.

"Thanks, Addison. Have a goodnight everyone." Jill pushes her way through the goodbyes and disapproving looks from the group. She continues on to the bathrooms before bravely walking out into a dark and foreign field. She comes to a very remote, chilled corner of the property. There she finds the single blue tent resting in solitude. She unzips the flap and crawls inside. As quick as she can, she pulls out her sleeping bag and burrows down within. She does her best to concentrate on falling asleep, trying to block out the ideas about her new friends, and the cold dark field, and Amsterdam, and farting in one's sleep. She tries to mute her thoughts, but they keep cycling around in her head. Amsterdam, to hot guys, to sexy accents, to Paris and the Eurail, to being alone, and back again to Amsterdam. One thought dominates the others, one thought is more insistent, while she lies there all alone, cold and shivering in a strange tent. "I want to go to Paris." Soon she finds the sleep she's been longing for.

.   .   .   .   .

Morning arrives, and Jill wakes to an empty blue tent. She looks over across from where she lay. A wrinkled green sleeping bag and a backpack similar to her own are squished into the corner, half buried under a crease of nylon. The vision of herself in this space, with the sad looking pile of Addison's worldly belongings make her feel lonely and rejected, and curious about where Addison and Mia might be sleeping. She decides not to hurry to find them. She wants to sit, wrapped up in her fleece sleeping bag, to be sad for a while, and use this time to process her emotions and position within the group. "They just left me here, out in the corner of the field all alone. No, I'm lucky to have such a nice person offer his tent for me to use last night. I'm being ungrateful." The thoughts rise and fall like the tides of an unsettled bay, and Jill slides deeper into the warm pocket of her sleeping bag. The warmth is no solution to the cold and she shivers and breathes short and quick, while the blood pumps from her heart to warm her extremities. "Nothing like a good hot shower to chase the chill and the blues away," she thinks.

Out of the lonesome blue tent, Jill emerges, clutching her cosmetics case and towel with frigid intensity. Halfway across the camping meadow she sees Mia. "Hey Mia!" She waves in discontentment, still disturbed by the isolation of the night before.

Mia comes jogging over to her friend. "You're going to shower? Hold on, I'm grabbing my things."

Mia returns within seconds, hugging a peach towel and a bag of cosmetics. "Jill, I'm so mad you ditched us to go to sleep last night!"

Jill smiles, trying to assess the mood and condition of her friend. "So, what happened after I went to bed?" Jill tries hard not to reveal that she's been hurt by the fact that she had to sleep in a weird tent all alone, all night long. It's a new day and a fresh start. What is there to complain about anyway? She's in Europe.

Mia frowns. "Oh, Jill, I really like Paul, but Addison wouldn't leave us alone for a second last night. It was a huge drag. We ended up just sitting around, crammed into Paul and Thomas's tent, talking all night. I'm so over Addison. I'm going to try hard to stay away from him today. What do you think about the two of us, with no guys, go out and explore today. I want it to be just us, Jill."

Jill nods her head, thankful to hear her friend's suggestion. She needs a break from the campground drama. It's a great day to reconnect and focus on why they've traveled so far.

"I love that idea Mia. After our showers, do you want to go grab an espresso and a yummy Dutch pastry?"

"Sounds perfect, Jill."

Together, side by side, the women carefully step across the final stretch of meadow and turn a corner into the bathrooms. Soon warmth and steam fill the concrete enclosure. The sound of water falling and splashing echoes across the tiled bathroom. The warm water is perfect for washing away dirt and insecurities.

Quatre

After a day of exploring and four different types of cake paired with hearty espresso, the women return to camp to find their men lounging and playing chess on the picnic table. Jill realizes it's been two full days, and it appears that these men are the only ones that use the desolate campground.

"There they are!" Mickey hollers, as he shoves Sean right off the picnic bench. He lands butt- first onto the cement patio.

"My girls have returned! We missed you, lasses," Sean shouts, laughing and pulling himself back up to the table.

"They're even crazier when they're sober," whispers Jill.

The redheads are there, too, and so is Addison.

"Well, I feel welcomed," Mia laughs. She whispers, "I'm just not sure I'm ready to hang out with them yet."

The two friends look into each other's eyes and nod, sharing a frame of mind. It's been a good day. Just the two of them, wandering around Amsterdam, taking pictures and talking about nothing important.

Then it happens. Thomas steps forward. He has the hood of his sweatshirt pulled over his head. He slips it back to properly greet Mia.

She gasps, putting her hand to her mouth, "You, you shaved your head!" She can't hide the disappointment in her voice.

"Do you like it?" He runs his hand across the close shaven stubble on top of his head.

"Why did you cut off all your hair?" Mia's world stops making sense, as she adjusts to Thomas (minus his shaggy auburn hair).

Jill is puzzled by the transformation as well. Before, Thomas looked nice, kind of like a young Irish Beck. Now, he looks like a squirrely, small-statured boy, who's lacking in skin pigment. Jill can tell that Thomas has just eliminated any shot he has at a romance with Mia. He can't compete now that he's lost his redhead appeal. The look of tragedy springs across Mia's face, as she sweetly smiles for him and tells Thomas his hair cut looks great.

Jill starts to laugh at Mia. Mia laughs too.

"Hi, Mia, did you have nice day?" Paul asks, before running his hand across a grove of red stubble that sprouts from his chin and jawline.

Before Mia can answer, Addison adds. "Mia, did you check out some of the café's I told you about? Was your day awesome?"

Mia sighs. "I think I want to take a walk." She gives Jill a look. Jill nods.

Sean asks, "Where are my little vixens walking too?" He gives the women a heavy flirtatious stare.

Mia wonders if Sean ever has a serious moment. "I think we're just going to walk over to the river, maybe over the footbridge." Mia points to the bridge and the road that passes above the water.

The two travelers leave the picnic table of men. Sean shouts after them. "Would you like us to come with you?"

"No, thanks, I need some time with my friend." Mia answers without looking back. The sun is starting to set and the mild temperature begins to drop. Jill and Mia increase their speed to keep themselves warm, hunching their shoulders in as they walk. Within ten minutes they're at the top of the footbridge below the overpass. They can see the campground, and the tents, and even the Irish men. They stand looking out at where they are in the world, thinking about the charming non-threatening men below.

"So, Jill, tonight when we go to the Red Light District, I want to get Paul alone. I think I'll have us split into groups. Can you help me distract Addison, so I can get some time alone with Paul?"

Jill nods. "Of course, I'll try, but he's pretty sprung on you."

"Hmmm, I know."

"Mia, do you remember what we were talking about earlier? Mia, I'm ready to go to Paris. I'm so over this right now. I'm dying to go see France."

Mia smiles with true affection for her friend. "I know Jill, I could stay a day or two more . . . but, for you, and for Paris, yes. Let's leave tomorrow." She looks a little deeper into Jill's sparkling eyes. "Don't you like our Irish men? Is there one that you like? I think you and Sean would make a cute couple."

Jill thinks of Mickey's handsome stature, blushes, and shakes her head. "I have my sights set on Paris."

"Well, okay, then." Mia reaches her hand out, and Jill puts her hand on top of Mia's. They turn around and head back to the camp to collect their escorts for the evening. A gust of wind blows right through them. Encouraged, the women dial up the pace.

The night develops, and seven Zeeburg campers find themselves unloading out of a large mini-van shuttle. Pouring into the shadowed streets, two blocks from the red light district. Addison is advancing closer to Mia, yet Paul seems to pull back from the competition some-what. This agitates Mia, and she becomes entirely distracted from experiencing the evening with her travel partner. Jill finds herself close beside Mickey and

Sean, which pleases her. She's in the perfect mindset to resign to let these goofy men tour the notorious district with her. Thomas is his usual quiet self, and his shaved head is tucked under a stylish brimmed hat. Everyone wears scarves and jacket with collars flipped up, shoulders squared, all are looking mysterious. The group stops in to a small, dimly lit café that sells an overwhelming selection of marijuana. The group crowds around one small raised table. Thomas goes and purchases some drugs. Paul rolls a joint. Jill laughs and takes a photo of his long pale Irish fingers rolling the paper methodically.

"I don't smoke weed," confesses Sean, who's starting to look nervous and squeamish.

"You don't smoke weed? What are you doing in Amsterdam, my Sean-bear?" Mia asks, before pointing and teasing him.

Jill puts her hand on his shoulder. "It's okay. I don't smoke either."

Sean gives her a wicked smile. "I will, if you will."

Jill's a sucker for a dare, and she already had decided that she would try smoking while in Amsterdam, just for the experience, and so she could say she had when back in the states.

The joint is passed around, and to both Mia and Jill's surprise, smoking is a bit more civil in Amsterdam. In the United States, binge smoking is encouraged. Huge bong hits, blunts, vaporizers, lots of THC are a common practice. In this group, everyone takes two little puffs off of a joint and are done. Jill thinks, "No problem, I can handle this." But after they leave the café and turn the corner to enter into the Red Light District she realizes she's starting to feel kind of funny.

Before she can argue, Mia gives them all orders. "Hey, let's split up. We can't walk down this way in such a big group. It's too obvious. We'll look like tourists."

As quick as she gives her orders, Jill finds herself left alone down a dark corridor in a strange place with Sean and Addison. Addison is a little stoned and it takes him a second to realize Mia's ditched him and is with Paul. The disappointment rushes across his face and can't help but hurt Jill's feelings. He's practically rude about the whole situation. After all, they share the same homeland and should stick together. It was Jill's wish to go see the infamous Red Light District, but now that they are here, she isn't so sure it's a place she wants to be.

"Come on, let's see if we can find them." Addison orders. He scans the street. Sean starts to giggle and is obviously not handling the THC well. Soon they're walking down a seedy, dimly lit street full of houses. All the houses are dark. Each house has great big windows with women standing in them, highlighted by a soft red light. They stand so still, like they're made of plastic. Jill can sense their eyes following her. She sees several men walking up and down the street. Then, she thinks of herself with Sean and Addison. One man walks up to her and says hello. He seems predatory and suspicious. She quickly grabs onto Sean, he responds by laughing hysterically. She draws herself close to him, wrapping her arm fast around his. Sean enjoys this, but is also absorbed in some "Sean party," all on his own.

"Look at this one!" Sean shouts to Addison. Addison tries to appear less preoccupied and stops to admire the woman in the window with Sean. Sean gently untangles himself from Jill. He steps forward to engage the woman. He points his finger up, and spins it around, to encourage her to turn and show him her backside. The seductive female doesn't move for a second, giving him the same stone-like expression. She turns herself around in a slow serpentine movement, flexing her legs which flow right into her stellar heels. She bends over for Sean. He starts howling with laughter. She turns again.

He mouths to her through the glass, "How much?"

He makes a money sign with his thumb and index finger. She takes a finger and curls it in, instructing him to come up to the door to negotiate. Then he points at her and starts to laugh. The woman scrunches up her eyebrows, looking displeased and possibly embarrassed. She glances at Jill to give her a look that says, "I feel sorry for you, if you're with this man." Jill hangs her head and the three continue down the shadowed street. Passing woman after woman, looking, and not talking. Jill notices they are being followed by an angry looking man in a trench coat. She clings on to Sean again, who's so high, he happens to be walking like he's drunk. Addison rushes ahead of them.

Caught between Addison's speed-walk, and Sean's drunk walk, Jill finds herself left behind with Sean who gives her no sense of protection or security thanks to his intoxicated state. At times he stumbles and she pushes up against him from the side to help him walk normally. The stumbling is drawing attention to them, and Jill wants nothing more than to find Mia, Mickey, Paul, and Thomas. "How did I get left with these two?" Jill thinks bitterly, as she shouts for Addison to wait for them.

Then at the end of the street, he calls out to her. "I found them!"

"Great, asshole, thanks for nothing,'" Jill thinks to herself.

The foursome look like they've had a more positive experience touring the Red Light District. Jill can't help but feel a small pinch of resentment. She's happy to pass Sean off to Mickey, who runs to his friend with loyal angst. The guys are immediately concerned about the state of Sean.

Mickey holds Sean by the shoulders. "Sean, what happened to you? What did you take?"

Sean laughs and says nothing. It seems as though he can't hold his own neck up at times, and his head just rolls to the side and hangs there.

Mickey addresses the group. "Okay, it looks like Sean's had his fun. Are we all ready to go back to the campground? Anything else anyone wants to do?"

Jill answers with certainty. "Let's just get back to the campground and drink some beer." She pulls her hair back and secures it in a tight ponytail.

"That's my girl." Thomas says, patting Jill on the shoulder. "What did you think of the Red Light District, sweetheart?" He gives her his full attention, awaiting her response.

Jill thinks for a moment. "Truthfully, Thomas, I'm kind of scared."

Thomas gives her a close look, then shakes his head. "Yeah, we kind of left you in incompetent hands. I'm sorry about that, Jill." Then he gives Addison a disapproving look.

Addison shrugs his shoulders.

All of the sudden Sean cries out in alarm before running as fast as he can straight into traffic; like he's being chased by something no one can see. Jill watches him head into the fast moving cars in the dark street. She screams, then turns away, unable to watch him get hit by a car. Everyone screams. The men are yelling his name to stop him. A car's tires squeal, and the smell of burning rubber marks the severity of what should have been the death of one very high Irishman. Mickey and Paul run out to grab him. They wave their arms to signal to the traffic, pulling him back to the sidewalk. The men guide him back to the group, where they circle around him. Everyone is shaking from the shock of witnessing him almost die. Sean is breathing erratically, his eyes are wide and he looks terrified. He's holding onto Mickey's forearm with both hands.

"What was that buddy?" Mickey asks, rubbing the shoulders of his unstable friend.

This question is followed by a chorus of "Are you okay? What happened? Why did you do that? And: you could have been killed."

Sean didn't know what he did. He asks Mickey to explain it to him twice on the cab ride back home. He starts breathing much better. The fright sobers the group and the mood shifts to embrace a more serious state of mind. They still gather at the picnic table in the dark, passing out cans of Henieken, and thanking God that Sean isn't dead.

Jill thinks, "This was just a freaking scary night. Everything about it was spooky. Tomorrow I am so going to Paris." With that, she wraps herself a little tighter into her coat, grabbing a beer to go, and saunters off into the darkness of the meadow without saying goodnight to anyone.

.   .   .   .   .

The next morning Jill collects all her belongings. She arranges them with precision in her backpack, then looks to the far corner of the tent where Mia softly sleeps.

She climbs out of the tent, looking back once to observe Addison sleeping in a corner, buried in a plaid lined sleeping bag. At some point last night, he and Mia must have come to bed in the tent. Jill's surprised to wake up and find that she had tent mates last night. It doesn't matter much, she's now pointing herself in the direction of Paris.

"Hey," she shakes the door of the blue colored tent. A gruff female voice answers, "Jill, I'll be out in two minutes." Jill hovers above the tent waiting. Shortly, Mia appears, crawling on her hands and knees. She looks hung over.

"Jill, I had the best time last night. We just hung out in Paul's tent and smoked." Several steps away from the tent, she adds: "I kissed Paul."

Jill notices the dopey love look that gives Mia's expression an instant face lift. She's practically gliding across the meadow.

"So, can we go to Paris now?" Jill's anxious to leave the campground and the drama. She thinks about their new friends, but just isn't invested enough to think too hard about them. Jill and Mia have a confirmed hotel room booked for several nights in Paris, and if they don't arrive tonight, they will have to pay for the room regardless.

Mia turns and looks back at the tents which are scattered and understated, glistening with morning dew. Then she looks out to the swift moving river channel, then back at Jill with a sigh. "Yes, we can go. I have

Paul and Thomas's phone numbers. They said we can call them if we need anything, or if we decide to come back."

"Well, we'll definitely be back for my flight home in eleven days. Don't worry, Mia, you'll see him again soon."

"Oh, I almost want to just stay here with them."

Jill's disturbed that her partner is willing to trade the adventure of a lifetime, to hang out with a random guy she just met. "What, are you serious? You know we're going to Paris right? Paris!" Jill tightens the straps on her shoulders, and fastens the hip belt of her pack. "Let's go already!"

Mia comes to her senses, and her eyes start to glaze over with romantic expectations for Paris. "Okay."

This time Mia is following Jill up the winding path that leads to the road, which takes them to the bus stop. Soon they're back at the bustling train depot, doing their best to decode the strange Eurail tickets. Today they must figure out which train will get them to Paris.

Jill takes a moment, and steps away from travel planning. She wants to soak in the images she's witnessing, trying her best to imprint them to her memory. This is her time in Amsterdam, and she hopes to seal the experience with at least a hint of understanding before leaving. She stares out across the expansive street which joins with a water way bearing old wooden ships that meet the city with history and mass. Windmills that tower above buildings, reminding the population of the rich culture and history of the region, and the vendors with little wooden carts, spilling over with brightly colored flowers. The colors and shapes of the tulips look like pieces of candy and come in shades she had no idea existed. The cobblestone streets that move to unknown places demand she look twice. She steps back, closing her eyes to listen and remember this.

Mia selects a train that will take them to Paris. Soon the two companions are rolling away from the depot, feeling tired and introspective, wondering what might be waiting at the other end of the line.

After a mix-up with the trains, and a short stop in Brussels, the women finally reach Paris. They eagerly step from the train platform and enter into a grand station. It's dark now, almost eight at night. The goal was to get to Paris, and that was as far as the plan went.

"So, where should we go?" Jill asks her friend.

Mia looks at the swollen crowd that scurries through the depot. She wants to scurry too. It seems natural. "Let's go find the metro and figure out how to get to our hotel."

The over-stimulated travelers manage to find a staircase that leads down to the metro station. In their hands they hold onto a map of the subway, the hotel reservation paper, and paper cups full of espresso they purchased from the concessionaire above

"Here, we want to get on the purple route," whispers Mia, using her fingers to help guide Jill with the translation of the map.

The metro station is bright and clean.

A tall, dirty hippie with dread locks approaches them. "Hi, are you two American?"

Mia and Jill nod in agreement.

"Have you been to Paris before?" The hippie tilts his head curiously, closing in on their personal space.

Jill steps back a bit, suspicious of his forward interest in them.

"Listen, you to have to be careful around here. Don't go out by yourselves at night. There are gypsies who like to find tourists to kill. They can harvest your organs and sell them on the black market."

Mia and Jill can't hide their distress. They stand frozen, unable to think of something to say to the crooked, smelly hippie. Jill tries to reason, "Was he messing with them, trying to scare them? Was he a con man and he's going to rob them? Was he just a nice traveler who wants to warn them of dangers? Was he telling the truth? What are gypsies?" She thinks of the Disney cartoon, "The Hunchback of Norte Dame," and thinks of the beautiful gypsy maiden who dances and wears big gold hoop earrings. This makes no sense, so she looks to Mia for answers and discretion.

Mia takes Jill's hand. "Okay, well, thanks for the warning, we're going to take this train now. Have a nice night."

The hippie man calls out, as they turn away. "Be careful!"

The women scramble onto the metro train, finding a nice bench seat far away from the handful of others who ride the Paris Metro. "He said not to go out after dark. Do you think that guy was telling the truth?" Jill asks Mia excitedly.

Mia can observe the fear based anxiety tip the scales of reason in Jill's mind. "Damn Jill, I don't know. I think he was just freaking crazy," she whispers just loud enough to be heard over the rumble of the speeding train.

Twenty minutes of waiting and finally their metro stop happens. Jill and Mia rush up the steep advancing staircase. As they move closer to the exit; the clean smell of fresh night air blows in from above, softening the rough edges. The thought of the creepy hippie and the nonsense of his warning are dismissed. They're heading up to meet their first encounter with Paris.

Once they reach the surface, and officially land in one of the most breathtaking cities in the world. The women discover the shock of arriving in the world's city. It's completely surreal. The two partners stand proud, clutching their heavy packs, beaming with the thrill of travel. They are taken back and it's not just the arrival to Paris, but the arrival of a milestone in life. Paris will undeniably change them, experience and culture is theirs.

"So, I think if we go this way, then turn right, and walk all the way up this street . . . we'll get there."

On the move again, the two gently tread down the Parisian sidewalk. Jill's surprised to discover they're in a residential area. The streets are quiet this time of night and lights from apartments shine down on them from high above.

"I figured our hotel would be in a tourist area. This is a nice neighborhood."

Mia answers as they walk. "I know it's strange here. I think I see a corner bar up ahead. Maybe we can go get a drink there tonight."

"Mmmm, French wine!" Jill shouts in anticipation.

Soon they find the hotel, which is more of a small bed and breakfast. The place is more upscale from the hostels, but still, nothing outstanding. Jill is glad they decided to upgrade from the hostels for their first few nights in Paris. The hotel is nestled in between two apartment buildings that are constructed with great similarity. From what Jill can tell, all the apartments are connected by some uniform design, and as the street curves, more and more windows with matching shutters or little balconies stretch out to make some sort of wonderful Parisian pattern. The only thing different, so one might distinguish one apartment from another, are the darling flower beds outside of windows hanging from random windows and cats curled up on balconies

.   .   .   .   .

It's a relief to be acquainted with their room. Two twin beds with floral bed spreads are pushed up against each side of the room. They have no closet, but the room does have a dresser and their very own bathroom. Jill is delighted to find that they now have one of the cute little windows with shutters on the outside and delicate lace curtains on the inside. Jill lies on her back on her bed. Mia stretches out on her back in her bed. It's decadence to be able to lay on one's very own bed in Paris, especially after sleeping on the ground in cold tents in Amsterdam for the past two nights.

"So, we should check out that corner bar, I guess. I think it's the only place to go to in this area," Jill's too excited to lay in bed for long.

"That place looks good. Can I shower first?" Mia calls out to her friend. She studies the crown molding that frames the ceiling.

Jill has her eyes closed to rest them. "You can, my friend. I'm so happy right now to just lie here. Can you remember the last time we were able to just lie down and do nothing? I can actually hear myself think!"

"Great! Keep thinking then, Jill."

The showers, fresh makeup, and clean clothes somehow give the women a renewed view of the evening. Paris is right outside and they can't resist the tremendous allure. The corner bar has little bistro tables scattered inside, and a few out front. It's now ten at night and the little bar looks clean and friendly with its bright lights and wrap around picture windows. The women walk in; dressed classy and looking fine. To their surprise they somehow find themselves struck by disappointment. On some level, they almost expect to see a group of handsome Irish men to greet them, happy, showering them with affection. Instead, there is no reception, and the two friends find themselves at the bar alone. Once again, the bar menu is confusing and hard to decipher. This time, there is no Heineken on the menu. The girls agree to try what seems to be the popular drink. "Can we have two glasses of that one? The sixteen, sixty four."

Within seconds two small glasses of amber colored drinks are sitting in front of the sheepish looking women.

"Mia, it's so quiet in here, like a library."

The women look around at the strange environment. The energy is so low, even the bartender greets them with insincerity. People are sitting in pairs, around little bistro tables, speaking in whispers or not talking at all, just smoking. This place is not conducive to socializing. As Jill looks around in silence, she wonders if these are the people who live in the quiet apartments with such uniformity. The resemblance between apartments is sort of enchanting in a way. All the pastel colors and the flowers hanging above sweet stone streets that bend and wind through storybook neighborhoods. Yes, these are the people who live here. They are quiet and reserved just like their homes. Then you have the Americans, as soon as the two walk into the bar, they need to make an entrance and be noticed. They want to make a statement. Even Mia who wants to fit in, and blend with the locals, wants those in the bar to notice her. This is not their scene, and after they sip away the expensive beer, they leave the corner bar to go back to their room to find a good night's rest in soft, warm, French beds.

All the way down, at the bottom of the hotel, in a strange dark room, waits breakfast. Jill and Mia are completely amazed by the delicious treats offered with their complimentary continental breakfast. The ability to wake up, and wander downstairs to meet a hot and tasty meal means more to Mia and Jill than any of the meals they've had so far in Europe. A dark room which looks like a dungeon enhanced by a fireplace, invites guests to go stand in line to take a plastic tray. Once one has their tray, they are given half a fresh baguette and an orange. To accompany the baguette, they set a small container of cream cheese and homemade strawberry preserves. Next each girl is given a steamy cup of thick hot chocolate. The fresh bread, hot chocolate, and sweet strawberry flavors are the women's first real taste of France.

"Oh, wow, I can't wait for tomorrow morning, so we can have this again," Jill says with delight. She empties her tray into a trash receptacle.

"So, are we going shopping today?" Mia gives Jill a mischievous look, before glancing around the room at the other tourists.

The debate has been going on since yesterday. Jill is so thrilled to be in Paris, she wants to do and see everything immediately, "The galleries? We could go see the Arc De Triomphe."

Mia pokes Jill in the side with her spoon, "Shopping!" she commands.

Jill decides she should accommodate her friend's wish first, then make her friend do all the crazy things she wants to do.

"Okay, Mia, I'll shop. Are you sure you don't want to go see the Eiffel Tower?"

"I do, but right now I have two hundred dollars that my dad gave me. He told me to buy a dress in Paris with it. I've been waiting three whole months to go find my Paris dress!"

"Okay, I agree. I want to shop, too. I need to find a perfect souvenir to take home. I want it to be a symbol of our journey."

"So let's grab our things, and find the shops!" Mia can't move fast enough.

"It looks like we want to go to Montaigne and Saint-Germain for the shopping district." Mia speaks out loud, while trying to piece together a plan of attack as she studies the subway map that has generously marked points of interest.

"Okay, I'm ready," announces Jill, as she carefully drapes two different cameras over her head, while simultaneously tucking her travel-pocket thing down her dress. Mia watches with discouragement at the spectacle of her friend who looks like she's doing some sort of weird magic act at a child's birthday party: tucking things, and looping things, and piling more things onto her singular body. She stands in front of her friend, armed and prepared for some sort of epic French battle. She's wearing a simple black dress, black tights and her black Maryjane shoes that she had packed to try to please Mia. The cameras and bulge of the undergarment pouch are too much. Jill needs both her cameras. The first camera being her big thirty five millimeter Canon with the zoom lens and black and white film. The second is a small digital camera for taking color photos. Mia finds herself stuck on her friend's appearance, thinking, "All that's missing is a bright red beret, and she'll look like the world's biggest tourist." Mia forces herself to disengage from the animated way her friend portrays herself. She decides to keep her cynical wisdom to herself. After all, this is Jill's dream, and there is no way Mia is going to stop her friend from taking in the city the way Jill needs to. Besides the pictures will be lovely.

Mia has her hair combed back behind her ears, and the faintest hint of makeup. She's wearing a delicate white blouse tucked into a simple pair of black slacks that hugs the curve of her hips. She holds a brown leather clutch, and stands with confidence in her Italian leather boots. She feels good and ready to explore.

Soon the two women find themselves emerging from a metro exit, standing in front of a brilliant Parisian intersection. Pedestrians dominate the streets and cars yield to the masses on foot. "Oh, Mia, Look! Starbucks. We have to go get a coffee. I'm dying for Starbucks."

"Jill, really? We can get Starbucks back home."

"Lighten up, Mia, if I want a Starbucks . . . it's okay to get a Starbucks. Besides, I'm a little homesick, and it makes me feel happy."

Jill isn't the only person who falls prey to the attraction of Starbucks. The two women stand in line for close to twenty minutes so Jill can order a grande iced caramel macchiato. "I paid almost eight dollars for this drink! Oh, it's so worth it Mia. Are you sure you don't want one?"

"I'll pass. I had too much sugar and coffee with breakfast this morning." Mia replies while trying to make a speedy exit away from the over the top corporate coffee shop.

The first store they enter is full of clothes for young women. It reminds them of the boutique stores in the malls back home. Trendy music and sullen mannequins striking modern poses advertise clothing that looks just like the styles back in California. Even though Mia tries hard to not act like such a tourist, in this particular situation she really needs to buy a dress that screams Paris. She needs a garment that she can take back home that will let everyone know that she shopped in Paris. This would be more than a dress, this is a statement. Jill's feeling open to finding something special too, but also needs her "find" to capture the energy and light that makes the city so special.

Moving on, they coast through two more shops, not finding exactly what they had imagined they would find, "I thought I'd find a certain style here, something new."

Jill nods, looking around, paying attention to what the local Parisian women are wearing. They seem to work hard to piece items together that fail to coordinate. The eclectic look is charming on them, but back home would easily be misunderstood. Yes, the look they saw many of the French women wearing seems unobtainable, or uninterpretable once taken out of context. Finally the women strike luck in one store. Mia settles for a frilled knee length skirt with browns and greens. She buys a bohemian, cream colored top to go with it, "It's not a dress, but I think its perfect Jill!"

"I think it was made for you, Mia. I'm glad you're happy."

Jill selects a tiny little coin purse in powder blue with pink roses near the clasps. "This is the perfect gift to bring back for my mom. It's small, so I can carry it in my pack, and it's affordable. Only twelve euros!"

After making their purchases, Jill and Mia tour some of the more iconic shops in the district, and as they pass the display cases with jewelry and purses; they don't even slow down. Jill feels as if they can't even afford to stand still to look at such notoriously expensive objects.

Outside of the shops, Jill discovers something that speaks to her more than anything they had seen all day. Across the street the spire of a gothic cathedral beckons and shows above everything else in the vicinity. For Jill, it's the first time she's seen anything like it, outside of a book. Jill believes this moment is a revelation. The massive structures symbolize so much for her, and had captured her imagination months before, when skimming through a text for her civilization course at the community college. The historic looking columns and French architecture tug at the frayed lines of her soul.

"Mia, we have to go see that!" Pointing at the cathedral, she uses her other hand to grab Mia's. Together they dash across the street to join clusters of tourists who gather outside to sit awhile on the steps.

Many photographs are taken, both black and white and digital. Minutes are spent contemplating and looking. The friends sit, soaking in the vibrations of the city. Feeling the tones and textures, the layers and rhythms that flow here. This is a place that balances both the new and the old. Progression and transgression, where all the great thinkers, artists, and martyrs collected and moved the populations, constructing the foundations that seem to cradle it all. A complex matrix of flavors and sounds. Gazing upon the rigid rock that somehow yields to the curve of a celestial vision. The sun grows heavy and slides down below the skyline of the city. Mia and Jill rise from their meditative state, and like the sun; move down a little lower to the tunnels of the metro.

"I'm so hungry Jill. Mia isn't satisfied with their crepe lunch from hours ago, and needs something adequate to replace all the calories spent on shopping.

"Here, let's try this one!" Mia points with a disciplined stature. She stands gesturing to a small, plain restaurant that barely maintains an entrance to the street.

"Sure, I'm starving," Jill responds and pushes her cameras to hang halfway tucked beneath her arm, instead of dangling dead center in front of her like she's been wearing them for the entire day.

Mia thinks, "Oh, thank God, she's making an effort to look less ridiculous. But then she realizes it's a simple misconception. She watches Jill take one hand and shove it down the top of her dress to fish out the traveler pouch. Mia realizes she isn't making an effort to blend in. Mia notices a few other people that are stuck; preoccupied with watching Jill adjust and readjust the two camera's and strange flesh colored pouch on a cord that all hang around her neck, resembling some sort of transient bondage. Mia squirms, and wishes to move on from this moment that refuses to pass. "Everything alright?"

Jill can detect the annoyed tone in her friend's voice, "You need dinner, Mia."

Mia shakes her head and rolls her eyes.

"It's true, so let's go get a table, grumpy," Jill directs, finally securing the dangling contraptions from her neck.

The women are greeted by a classy looking female who's working as the restaurant hostess. She takes the two tired travelers to a charming little table for two, tucked around the corner from the entrance. Inside the restaurant; the walls are a dark brown and the carpet a dirty beige. A serious and bored waiter approaches with menus. He's obviously not impressed with Americans. When Mia asks him for water, he averts his eyes and leaves without saying a word. He leaves two French menus behind. Jill's eyes drop down as she does her best to understand the menu. She can't pronounce the name of the restaurant, let alone pick out food from words she has no clue about. She knows escargot are snails, so she makes a point to make sure to eliminate anything that might sound like escargot. She scans over the thick papered menu until she finds something familiar. It's a word she recognizes from Amsterdam.

Soon the brazen waiter with the thick black eyebrows reappears and seems even more irritable than before. He splashes a pitcher of warm water on the table, and sets two glasses down. He pulls out a pad and a pen from his apron and gives Mia a look that permits her to give him the order.

"I would like the croquet madame."

'Yes, fine. Anything else for you?" He gives Mia a look that gives her doubts about her order. She shakes her head. Then he turns to Jill. "And for you?"

Jill opens her menu and points to the words as she reads them to him. He just stares down at his pad, trying his best to tolerate the slow dimwitted style of the tourists.

"I would like the de terres frites, and the pommes de terre au fromage." She mispronounces almost the entire order, and as she gives it to the waiter, it feels more like a question than a request.

He raises his black furry eyebrow at her. "Anything else for you? Okay, mademoiselle, merci." The icy man, is gone, disappearing into the darker quarters of the restaurant that mingle with the silent, but good smelling kitchen.

"Whoa, that was intense. Mia, we just met an actual rude French waiter! Have you heard of that stereotype before? That's the funniest thing ever!"

Mia's gazing past two other tables of couples and out into the street. She lets her eyes relax and doesn't focus on anything specific.

"Are you thinking about Paul?" Jill whines, trying to coax her friend out of her daydream so that they can enjoy a proper Parisian meal together.

Mia smiles, "I am. What if we go back to Amsterdam, spend a few more days there? I mean, after we see Paris of course."

"What? No way. Paris is way better. We haven't even seen anything yet. For example, look!" Jill points out the window to someone passing by. The person is going slow and gazing in at them as they gaze out.

"What? That homeless woman?" Mia gives Jill her attention, curious about what her friend thinks she sees.

"That's not just a homeless woman. That's a French bum, Mia. A real French bum. Look at her! She's way more classy than the bums we have back in the States. Look, she has a shawl. A real shawl, like the bums in movies and stuff."

Mia starts to laugh, and Jill joins her. The French bum pauses, she's aware of the dining women's cruel laughter while they watch her. Her eyes moisten and glisten, the only tell that she's a real person with feelings. The rest of her face remains stone-like. When the American tourists see the pained expression, they laugh even harder.

A minute later, they're interrupted by the impatient server. Without a word, he comes to the table and slams down the plates of food in front of the women. "Anything else for you?"

Jill and Mia shake their heads in submission, and wait for relief to arrive. He walks away, leaving them to their intimate little dinner. Mia has a small ham and cheese sandwich on crusty toasted bread with a fried egg on top. It's Jill's dinner that has the two women confused and delighted.

"Oh, Jill, you didn't!" Mia whispers, leaning in over her plate.

Jill sits with two plates in front of her. On one plate she has a baked potato with some cheese melted on the top. On the other plate she has a nice grouping of French fries. Two smiles equally push up at the corners of their inquisitive faces. "You didn't!"

"I didn't mean to." Jill answers defensively.

"Jill! I can't believe you ordered a baked potato with a side of French fries! How did you do that? You didn't do it on purpose, did you? What were you trying to order?"

"I don't know," Jill shrugs her shoulders with embarrassment, but then joins in with her friend to have a good laugh over the unfortunate dinner selection.

"So, can I have some of your sandwich? I'll give you some fries."

"Jill, stop being a French bum and eat your de terres frites."

"Whatever. You know you love being a tourist. Embrace it, be it, own it," Jill cheers quietly, trying hard to pull Mia's thoughts from the Irishmen who are only a train ride away.

Jill continues, speaking in between bites of potato, "It's good, isn't it? To be here in Paris? I'm starting to get a sense of the city. I can't wait for tomorrow. We're going to the Louvre tomorrow, no matter what. Imagine it, Mia. To actually be able to look at the Mona Lisa. I mean, we're going to actually see the most famous and mysterious pieces of art in the whole world! Us! We are, Mia!"

Mia starts to giggle with excitement, watching her friend describe her tourist dreams in such a romanticized way. The waiter passes by and pulls the empty plates from the table. He returns after a long pause, then drops the check. The women count out coins, and figure in a tip, then leave the Euros in a pile on top of the tab.

"Math is tricky in Euro's. I keep trying to figure out the conversion, to understand what we're actually spending on dinner!" Mia complains light heartedly.

Interactions and transactions have been increasingly challenging over the course of their first week in Europe.

Cinq

The first full day in Paris has passed. The women meet the morning with another free breakfast.

"Out of all the food we've had in Europe, I love these continental breakfasts best. I had no idea baguettes with cream cheese on them tasted so delicious." Jill declares between hungry nibbles of bread.

"Ha! Jill, that's because this is the only food we haven't picked out for ourselves. We need someone local to teach us how to eat around here." Mia's point is well taken, and it makes Jill wonder what other kinds of amazing foods they're probably missing out on, just because they have no idea they exist.

The other tourists are equally bubbly and happy in the dark underground dining room. The energy is ideal. People sit, anxious and ambitious, preparing for another perfect day in Paris. Jill likes the vibe, it's less formal. People can relax and not worry too much about cultural mannerisms.

"So, the question is: is this our last night in Paris before we move on tomorrow morning, or do you want to stay a fourth night?" Mia asks. She leans in, over the table. The women intentionally kept their itinerary loose. Only planning options to feel out the progress of their adventure.

Jill looks conflicted, "I don't know. Honestly, I'm not sure what I want to do. I love it here, but I'm dying to go see Switzerland too."

"Well, we can try to see Notre Dame this morning, since I know that's really important to you, then we can go to the Louvre . . . see, they're almost within walking distance." She points to the metro map. "I think. Then, if we do both, we'll be able to head out to Switzerland in the morning. Oh, wait, I wanted to see the Eiffel Tower. We have to see the Eiffel Tower!" Mia says, glad to solidify a schedule out loud.

"Well, the Eiffel Tower will look gorgeous at night, it's covered in lights." Adds Jill.

"Perfect. Then let's take the metro to Notre Dame. Walk to the Louvre. Then catch a cab to the Eiffel Tower to have dinner nearby."

Jill stands up, "That sounds like the best day ever. Let's go already."

.   .   .   .   .

Emerging from another subway tunnel, Jill and Mia are taken aback by yet another vision, compliments of Paris. When Jill spies the gothic point of a cathedral reaching up towards the powers that be, her heart is overcome with awe and gratitude. Catholic roots that run deep, flex within her. She feels her whole being lured closer, called to the immense fortress that house the many secrets, histories, and shadows that stem from her religion. Her connection to this place is instantaneous. She's moved by all the other tourists who come to pray and pay homage to the wonder that is Norte Dame. Even non-believers hold a fascination for the legacy of this church. Jill feels emotion pooling within, and she hasn't even entered through the great arched doors. She's unsure if she can, fearing her legs may buckle from under her before they make their way inside. This is enough; to come this far and be this close.

Mia tucks her arm inside of Jill's. "Jill, it's beautiful. I'm so glad you insisted we see this."

Jill squeezes her companion's arm a little tighter. "Wait, I'm not ready to go in yet. I just need to walk around this. I want to see the outside. I need to photograph it."

So, while droves of visitors line up and enter through the front doors, Jill takes Mia on a walk around the perimeter, stopping every couple of paces to try to get a close look at a gargoyle, or an intricate trim around a window pane. Mia starts to lose interest and Jill hesitates, feeling that her time with this place is limited. She knows the right thing to do is to accommodate her friend. So, in they go, following a procession of well-caffeinated, pastry-stuffed tourists.

The tourists make the women feel a little more comfortable, and they feel a little less inhibited once inside the historical structure. Statues and bells, vaulted ceilings and stone walls hold and protect a collection of stained glass that is so incredible, they speak novels all their own. Jill is searching for something inside of Notre Dame. She isn't sure exactly what she's looking for, but she can't deny she craves something. She feels a pressure push upon her thoughts, just outside of a definitive range. With each step, deeper into the cathedral, the common things become fuzzy and fall from her focus. Even Mia seems distant, despite the fact that she is right beside her. She thinks, "Perhaps at the end, when I reach the altar, I'll find it." She wants some sort of encounter. She needs this place to give meaning to her trip and to somehow affect her. Solemn and humble, she proceeds, peering around corners and studying the details where the walls meet the floors.

In the end, what she found, was what she had. She walked through the church, took dozens of black and white photos, found a pew to rest in and pray, meditated on the stained glass kaleidoscope of imagery and eventually turned to her polite and somber friend who was also enjoying her own peace, within the walls of Notre Dame, "Should we go?"

Mia nods her head. The two rise from their deep moment, sidestepping out from the middle place of a central pew.

Mia looks at Jill. "This is good. I'm really glad we came here this morning." She winks at Jill.

"Me, too."

Outside and over a river, the sun shines down and the traffic moves at a quicker pace than before. They're about a twenty minute walk from the Louvre.

"Ice cream?" Mia points at an ice cream shop up the street.

One coffee ice cream, and one pineapple ice cream later, and the women relish their decadent stroll through Paris. Soon they reach the Louvre, and continue their journey on foot through the levels and different wings that segregate by centuries, popularity, and mediums. First the oldest relics. Pieces so old, that just their mere existence laments to Jill and Mia that there were cultures and beliefs long ago. All that may be left of them, are here, in a small collection of bone carvings and cave drawings.

Hours later, the two gallery patrons have finally entered into a new level of the museum. Mia stops short, gawking and blinking her eyes at the sight of something glittering down a quiet hall, "Oh, my god! Jill look. It's the Crown Jewels."

Jill gasps, "I've never seen anything like it in my life."

Both women can feel their mouths salivate while standing so close to such a monumental collection of rubies, emeralds, sapphires, and diamonds. Each piece is more hypnotic and fantastic than the next. Jill has to force her hands to her sides to resist the impulse to press them to the glass. She isn't a huge fan of jewelry, but the presence of these particular jewels are undeniably irresistible.

"I've never been the type of girl to feel emotional over a piece of jewelry . . . but, my God!" Mia whispers, while referencing the watchful eyes of the silent and ever-so-still museum staff.

"I don't even want to blink. Like, if I stare hard enough into this giant ass diamond, I" change somehow!" Jill replies.

Jill and Mia giggle, then summon enough strength to walk out of the bedazzling sanctuary, breaking themselves away from the intoxicating way the jewelry captivates.

More great works, after great works trail down halls, that lead to other halls. Jill's been dreaming of this visit for months, and she can't believe she's actually inside of this building. Surrounded by so many phenomenal mediums of art. Monet, Van Gogh, Renoir and Picasso are all there. Preserved within the masterpieces seem to be the essence or a small remnant of the creator's soul. It's her chance to meet them, and know them on this superficial level. Art this good transcends time, life and death. The brush strokes and mineralized pigments lay out movement and feeling that can only be described as a concentrated reflection of a culture. It's us, captured in time, and hung on a wall to last through the decades. Resting beyond cycles of generations.

And here's Jill, she made the great pilgrimage over the ocean to come and see them for herself. Words escape both women, and all that can be heard are the slow steady footsteps through hallowed halls.

Free to roam and discover, the women allow themselves to become seduced by this world dripping with perfect art. They walk and look, and walk some more, until their feet ache and their eyes give them headaches from staring too hard.

"My brain hurts from processing all this art. Should we go find something to eat and take a taxi to the Eiffel Tower?" Mia chimes, still partly swayed by the presence of good art.

"Yes! I think I saw a crepe stand in the park outside. Near the big arch. I'm so hungry, I'm having two crepes. One with mushrooms and cheese, and the other with chocolate," Jill responds with determination.

"Jill, we've been here for six hours!"

"I know," Jill smiles with pride. "There's still so much more. You have to promise we'll come back here."

"Sure Miss Jill. Let's go find our crepes. I'll buy you an espresso. Yy treat."

In the park, the vibe is immediately different. It's a bright spring day in Paris and everyone's outside doing nothing. Just like in a movie, there are young children launching little toy sailboats into a fountain, painters with easels trying to capture the light, and lovers wrapped up in each other's arms sprawled out on picnic blankets. They move past an old man throwing bread crumbs to pigeons, eyes focused on two young men flying bright red kites.

"Jill, look," Mia sighs. She raises her arm and points her finger rigid and firm to something special off in the distance.

"The Eiffel Tower! It's so close, Mia. Do you think we could try to walk there?"

"Hmmm, you know, we can try. It's hard to tell how far away it is. A mile, maybe two. We can walk, and if we need to call a taxi, we can. One way or another, we're going there tonight!"

"Sounds like a plan of gold." Jill replies, turning her gaze to the man with the crepe stand.

Mia and Jill find a quiet little bench under a Parisian tree to feast on crepes, relax and watch the city.

"I've gotten pretty good at ordering these Pain au Chocolats! I swear they're the best thing ever." Jill pops the last bite of her croissant, then lifts her heavy cameras from around her neck. She carefully places them in between herself and Mia. "Will you watch my cameras for a second? I'm going to check out the stand right there. I need to get a closer look at those tee shirts."

Mia sweetly agrees, but as Jill stands up to walk over to the booth, Mia gives the cameras a sneer of detest. All over Paris, the two obnoxious cameras have been following her. If they could go out just once in Paris without the big embarrassing cameras, Mia would feel so much more tolerant. But then she looks up, and sees her friend so genuine and full of innocence. It really is a joy to see her so happy and inspired. Back home, Jill wasn't as energized. Mia's happy to see the transformation within her travel companion.

Jill comes running back to Mia, she has a blue plastic bag with a white Eiffel tower on the side. "Look what I got! I know it's cliché, but . . . it sums it all up for me!" Jill set her eyes on Mia, anticipating Mia's look of panic, because Jill has just elevated herself another notch on the dorky tourist meter. Out comes a big black hooded sweatshirt with bright white words that read "I (heart) Paris".

Mia laughs, "It's you, Jill, all the way."

"Oh, yeah, I'm glad you feel that way because I'm going to put it on right now!"

"Oh," Mia whimpers.

On goes the big black sweatshirt with the words and the red heart, and then, back on go the cameras.

"Wait, give me that," Mia swipes the bigger black and white camera. "Here stand by the fountain, I can get the Louvre in the background behind you."

Mia and Jill swap cameras and spend the next thirty minutes enjoying an impromptu photo session. After the espresso is drunk, they submit to the allure of the Eiffel Tower.

Down one block, then they turn and proceed up another block. In the distance the tower still looms, and it appears they haven't gotten much closer. The sun is starting to set, their pace quickens. People who are getting off work start to fill the streets, they too roust a quick pace. Thirty minutes of walking passes and both women are growing tired and anxious. They can see the tower as it teases and taunts, but almost like a mirage, every time they think they're going to reach the street that leads to it, the tower seems a little further away.

"I guess it was further than I estimated," Mia scoffs, folding her arms across her chest while walking.

"It's okay, I don't mind. It's the walk of a lifetime, right? We're walking to the Eiffel Tower! It just doesn't get any better!" Jill boasts, in between deep pants from the vigorous movement.

After forty-five minutes of devoted trekking, they arrive. Beneath the great edifice, Mia and Jill stand; looking completely overwhelmed by the very famous symbol of French culture. Then the lights come on. A gasp of wonder exhales from the crowd of sight-seers. The tower twinkles and sparkles.

Mia and Jill are so tired from Nortre Dame, The Louvre, and the walk to the tower that their feet ache just looking at so many flights of stairs to the top. So, they opt to enjoy the tower from the ground. While posing for pictures and trading off the cameras, a handsome French man walks up to Mia.

"Hi."

Mia squirms with awkwardness and surprise, "Hi."

Jill stands, snapping a picture of the exchange.

"Are you two girls American?"

Jill walks over to join Mia, since she's been included in his question. "Yes," she boasts with pride."

"Those are my friends over there." He points to four dashing Frenchmen who step forward from the crowd. The men wave.

"I am on a . . . how do you say? a, bachelor party. I am getting married tomorrow." He talks low, with an earthy French accent.

This is when things start to heat up and the women can't help but swoon. He gets down on one knee, like he's proposing to Jill and Mia both. He turns and gives his groomsmen a fast grin, before continuing. Puzzled, the women listen and watch, anticipating what the groom will do next.

He looks up at them with kind, dark eyes, "I have to perform several things tonight as part of the celebration. Umm, sort of a scavenger hunt. One of the things I have to do, is to find two American girls to kiss me under the Eiffel Tower." He clears his throat, looking serious and endearing. "So, would you both be kind enough to give me a kiss?" His cheeks turn red with embarrassment.

"We would be happy to!" Mia answers, delighted by the fun party game.

The French groom stands up. Jill leans in on one side, while Mia leans in on the other. The groomsmen close in, pulling their cameras out, shouting things in French and laughing with pleasure. On the count of three, the girls both kiss his cheeks. The deed is recorded on film. Then to their surprise, he turns and kisses Mia's cheek, then Jill's cheek.

"Thank you so much, girls. Have a wonderful night in Paris. I really appreciate this!"

His groomsmen wave goodbye, and they are gone as fast as they had surfaced. Now, Mia and Jill are both completely kissed over the edge. Totally submerged in the warm and romantic way Paris can make one feel. Something about the Eiffel Tower, Paris at night, and a man in love who was giving away kisses, has them both pleased and stirred by their Parisian experience.

"Should we call a cab?" Jill asks Mia.

"I don't know. I kind of feel like going for a walk. Look at all these people out enjoying the night. The whole city is lit up in this area. What about over there?" Mia responds, taken by the seduction of the city.

"I'm glad you said that. I want to walk a little more, too. I can't believe he kissed us! Under the Eiffel Tower, we got kissed! Mia, I think we can call our day a success." Jill lifts her camera and snaps another photo of her friend. They walk and look, and keep walking.

The day and the night feel so vivid. Mia doesn't even mind that her friend who's walking beside her is wearing a giant "I heart Paris" sweatshirt with two cameras and a travel pocket dangling from her neck. Even the cameras seem perfect, because, at first, Mia thought Jill didn't get it, but after today, she realizes, maybe "she's the one whom doesn't get it." Jill knows how special this place is, and she knows she's a tourist here. She embraces these facts, and it works to her advantage. She wants to record everything and be herself in contrast to a different kind of backdrop. Mia realizes, it might just be okay. Who cares if people may laugh at them. This is their experience. Jill chooses to do it the way she's envisioned for herself. Mia decides maybe it's not so bad.

Tonight they don't stop at a bar. Instead, they quietly and soberly make their way back to the hotel. In the morning, it will be time to leave Paris.

Six

Morning creeps in waves, blazing on the creases of the white bed sheets. Jill and Mia gleefully pack, then repack their things into their overstuffed backpacks. Final showers are taken. The next shower opportunity may not occur until they secure some sort of lodging that awaits in Switzerland.

"One more incredible free breakfast!" Jill cheers with an authoritative zip of her pack. "Are you ready to check out?"

"I'm as ready as I'll ever be," Mia playfully responds. She scans the room one last time.

"I'm so excited to see Switzerland! The mountains and lakes. I think it might just be the most gorgeous place I'll ever have the privilege to visit."

Mia nods her head. She always falls quiet to listen to the way her friend describes things and experiences. She loves the way Jill has the ability to project how she relates to something simply by using her words. Jill has a unique way of looking at things.

Soon, the two check out and head to the train depot. This time, they have to locate a different train station on the opposite side of Paris. Trying to understand the metro system so that they can locate the new station takes a little longer than expected. Dealing with the Eurail pass is also a challenge, and neither woman has mastered these transactions completely.

Brave, and on a mission, the two step forward, holding out their passes in order to secure the train out of France. Passports and tickets in hand, they board a high-speed train. Amazement and delight are shared as they find an empty train car all the way at the end of the long train.

"Oh, thank God, I can take a nap here. I'm still tired from all the sight - seeing from yesterday." Jill drops her bag in an empty seat.

Mia sets down her pack with precision on the floor across from her. "Yeah, I think we should have scheduled at least five or six days to really get to know Paris. We tried to do and see too much yesterday. Let's do Switzerland differently."

Jill sits down, propping her feet against Mia's pack. "Well, we have four more trips on our Euro Rail pass. We can skip Lourdes and spend more time in Zermatt or Paris."

"Or Amsterdam." Mia reminds Jill, unable to let go of her desire to see Paul.

Mia shifts into a comfy orange seat. She stretches out her legs. "Yeah, I do want to see more of Paris. I'm sad that we're leaving her right now." Mia stretches her arms up above her head, pulling and loosening her tense muscles. "So, Jill, we didn't book any place to stay tonight in Geneva. Are you sure we'll find a place?" Mia's voice lowers an octave as her thoughts transition from Amsterdam to the unplanned plan.

"I'm completely sure. We'll just get directions to the nearest hostel from the train station people. I'm not stressing about that at all. I'm just kicking back, and going to look out the window. I'm just going to watch the countryside pass by. We can relax. It's a long train ride. We can worry about all that when we get there."

Mia stares at her friend, trying to read her body language and detect the authenticity in her demeanor. She seems way too laid back, considering they have no place to go when they reach the next country. Passes are punched and soon the train starts to move. The first hour is fascinating; the second is also pleasant; by the third hour, both women fall asleep. Several people enter the train car at multiple stops, and as the train continues, they eventually disappear, leaving only Mia and Jill.

"Jill, wake up."

"Wuh, huh?"

"Jill, you're snoring way too loud."

"What? I don't snore."

"Yeah, look; you're also drooling." Mia starts laughing, and points to a wet spot on the back of the seat where a pool of saliva's been collecting. Jill wipes her mouth and blinks her eyes hard a few times.

"What time is it? I think it's close to five. I heard we'll be there in another forty five minutes. But, really . . . be where? Jill, do you really think we'll find a hostel?" Mia wants to prepare, or simply have some sort of a vague plan to build off of.

"Well, even if we can't find a hostel, I'm sure there are hotels. Geneva's a really big city in Switzerland. We'll be fine. What should we do for dinner tonight?"

The crackers, cheese, and mineral waters from the train hardly counts as lunch.

"We haven't had a proper meal since California." Negative thoughts cloud Mia's confidence.

By the time the train pulls into the depot, the girls have already gathered all their things and are looking forward to getting off the train so they can meet Switzerland. The sun is setting, and the elevation feels higher. Geneva hugs a lake and the temperatures are brisk.

"This is even colder than Amsterdam." Jill breathes inward.

"No comparison. I'm freezing!" Mia answers, just before pulling out a wool scarf from her bag. She wraps it around her neck several times.

Jill starts to laugh at her friend. For the first time it's Mia who looks funny. She has an old blue sweatshirt, a faded brown scarf, her pack, plus she's hunching over from fatigue and the cold. She looks so haggard and downtrodden, a twenty year old hobo, wandering about Switzerland with no place to go. Jill starts to laugh even louder. Mia laughs, too.

The absurdity of the situation doesn't escape them, and when they peer out of the depot, they realize they have no idea what to do.

"There's a café down the street. I see pizza!"

"Perfect!" Jill replies.

After settling into a little bistro, their packs shoved in tight below the table, the women assimilate and rest while loading up on hot greasy carbs.

"These miniature beers are starting to annoy me." Jill says, while twisting the bottom of her glass back and forth between her thumb and index finger.

"Yeah, they kind of suck," agrees Mia. "So, we've had our pizza and beer, it's time to go find this hostel."

"I asked the server, and she said it's only two blocks down from here."

"I'm seriously so tired of trying to find places, Jill. Can't we just stay there." Mia points across the street at a giant towering hotel that has lights wrapped around the exterior giving out a golden glow. Jill studies the building with a forlorn expression.

"I think that place is way too expensive."

"Jill, at this point, I don't even care. I would pay two hundred dollars right now, for a nice room."

"Whatever, I think we should go check out the hostel."

The hour passes, and the evening has a way of sucking the fun from the girl's adventuresome spirits. They're no longer thrilled to be in Switzerland, but they're well fed, and now, are in need of a quiet bed to lay in. Jill senses the urgency in Mia's disposition. They collect their packs, leave a modest pile of cash on the table for the pizza, and hobble down the street in search of the infamous hostel. Just like the server said, the hostel is exactly where it should be. The walk is even downhill, which lightens the weight contained in their packs.

Mia yelps with happiness, then hands off her backpack to Jill. "I'll be right back, mi compadre'!"

A minute later, Mia comes charging out of the hostel looking irritated and angry.

"What's up?" Jill asks, concerned and confused.

Mia gives Jill a look that could kill. "Yeah, your hostel Jill, it's full. They have no beds for us. What are we supposed to do?" Mia's face turns from mad to fearful. "Aaaah, I'm just so freaking tired, Jill. That's it. We're going back to that fancy hotel by the depot."

Jill knows not to press Mia right this second. She knows that if Mia needs a fancy hotel room, then that's what they need to go find.

Fifteen minutes later, and one grueling walk uphill back to the depot, the worn women stand in front of the grand Swiss hotel. "Oh, Jill, we've been walking in circles. Hold on, I'll go in and find out how much it costs."

Jill nods her head and decides to let her companion do the travel negotiating. After several minutes, Mia comes walking out of the elevated abomination; looking defeated and conflicted.

"What's up?" Jill asks, picking up on the unsettled way her friend now seems.

"Umm, Jill . . . they have rooms."

"Sweet!" Jill scoots up to give her friend a high five.

"Yeah, no." Mia sidesteps to dodge the raised up hand. "It's four hundred and fifty dollars a night."

Jill leans forward and gently sets her hand on Mia's shoulder. "Mia, I know you're so tired and need a room. These are way too expensive, but, because we are a team, I'm happy to stay there . . . if that's where you need to be tonight."

A look of doom and defeat smears across Mia's long- traveled face. "We're so screwed. We should have stayed in Paris. This is just so messed up, Jill. What are we supposed to do? Mia shifts her weight from one foot, and then back again to the other foot. She looks up the street, then turns and looks back down the street, shaking her head in anger.

"It's not that bad, Mia. We're fine. Look." Jill points to a group of young adults in their twenties walking past the train depot to an upper deck area. Mia looks, and waits for Jill's suggestion. "Listen."

Mia listens, standing still with her ears perked, mimicking her friend's action. Music is playing from somewhere far away. It sounds like rock music, and seems to be coming from the direction that the group of twenty something's are headed too.

Jill smiles, hoping and praying that wherever the music is, it will somehow throw them a life-line, and lead them to somewhere good. It's close to eight, but the streets and the train station are empty compared to Paris. Geneva is a big city, but also a quiet city.

"So, let's go find this music, and maybe hang out and get a beer or something."

Mia just stares at Jill, disappointed in the incomplete plan.

"Hey, we met the Irish guys at a bar, and they were happy to help us. I'm sure there are really nice Swiss people at a bar nearby who will be helpful after they hear of our predicament."

"Predicament?" Mia starts to laugh. She squeezes the straps of her pack tightly, and turns to follow Jill toward a staircase in the corner of the train station. Soon they find the music, the young people, and a bar. Jill and Mia linger outside of the dark, small space before summoning the courage to make their way in. Most of the time Mia is proud to be carrying her seasoned backpack, but tonight she feels awkward and can't appreciate the bulk of her luggage attracting attention.

"Here, let's go." Jill opens the little windowed door for Mia. It takes several seconds for their eyes to adjust to the dimly-lit bar. Both women resemble deer caught in a headlight, stunned and unsure of what they are about to do, unaware of where they're trying to go.

"A pool hall!" Jill exclaims, feeling a little more comfortable.

Mia observes the room. It's divided into two parts. One side contains a simple crowded bar with a bathroom off to the side. The other half of the room has four large pool tables. A group of six, posh-looking friends are sitting on a nearby couch, visiting. Two of the pool tables are being used by other twenty-somethings. Mia's posture relaxes, she stops squeezing the straps of her pack.

"Beer?" Mia whispers to Jill. "What do you think, pool?"

Jill's relieved that Mia's embracing the side-tracked circumstance. She can see the tension fall from her partner's face; they're both able to find comfort in this godsend of a pool hall. "Yes, don't worry. I'll go up and get us a couple beers and ask about the pool tables."

Mia nods and stands off to the side, trying to press herself up against a dark brown wall. She watches the other pool players. One game consists of couples playing against one another. Two women and two men. Mia watches them with interest, trying to assess their style and culture. The other table has only two players, two men who are in the midst of an intense game.

Mia watches the Swiss pool players, hearing the clunk of the cue tip hitting the cool white ball. She allows herself to daydream for a moment, recalling the night they met the Irishmen, and the warm affectionate game of pool they all shared. She remembers how she slyly leaned far over the table, aiming her stick to knock the colored balls into the desired pockets. She exaggerated the angles, and used the pool stick as a prop, to make herself look a little more enticing. Her audience was receptive.

Jill stands at the bar patiently. The bartender is a tall ash-blonde woman, possibly in her thirties. She has her hair pulled back in a ponytail and is wearing a black leather vest over a black tank top. She stops and serves two other people before coming to Jill last. "Hi, can I get you something?" The blonde asks in English.

"Hi, I"ll have two of your cheapest beers, and I want to play pool." Jill stammers, feeling nervous and shy.

The blonde climbs halfway over the counter to get a little closer, so that Jill can hear her over the loud pulse of the music. "Sure, it will be thirteen dollars, and you get the pool table for forty five minutes."

"Oh, okay," Jill said looking dissuaded by the potential for an expensive evening in the bar. She starts to fish for her traveler pocket, hand over hand, pulling it out of the front of her sweater. The bartender's beginning to look impatient. She raises her eyebrow as she tries to recognize the weird purse this tourist carries under her clothes. She tips it upside down to shake out the strange Swiss coins. She had converted some Euros into the Swiss currency back at the Paris train depot. She holds the little dime-like coins in the curve of her palm, staring as they glisten in the light from the bar. The bartender starts to look irritated and keeps turning to acknowledge others who are waiting at the other end of the bar. Jill hesitates as she starts to push the coins back and forth in her palm, trying to figure out values. Finally she takes a big breath, and holds them out to the blonde.

The bartender looks at Jill and smiles. "Okay, don't worry." She counts out a few of the little dimes, then disappears for several minutes before reappearing with two small beers and the pool balls.

Jill's face lights up, reveling in her first Swiss transaction without Mia's assistance. She beams as she collects the two beers, carrying them to Mia. She returns to retrieve the pyramid of colored balls. The Americans timidly make their way along the border of the dark room until they claim a table of their own. Mia sets their drinks on a small shelf next to the pool table. Jill goes over to pick out some nice billiard cues. Mia sets the balls up on the table. She instructs Jill to break.

"I'm so missing our boys right now. We should just go back to Amsterdam." Mia shares, before knocking a ball across a bed of felt.

"No way. We're in Switzerland. Do you know how cool that is? Give this a chance. You'll love it."

Mia frowns at Jill and her defense of the forsaken place. This wasn't Amsterdam, and it wasn't Paris. After visiting such action-packed cities, Geneva couldn't help but fall short in Mia's opinion.

Mia and Jill both feel the unfriendly vibe radiating from the rest of the bar patrons. It feels like the two women are being tolerated, but not encouraged in this dim, slow-going kind of bar. The music has too much distortion, Jill suspects it must be close to a decade old.

"Hold on, Mia. I'm going to the restroom to pee."

With their packs tucked underneath the pool table, Jill walks boldly through the bar, fondling the nylon cord of her traveler pocket. Once inside a stall painted a dark shade of red, Jill's mind begins to race, reviewing their grim situation. She needs to come up with a plan before Mia gets bored with the pool hall. What can they do? She hears two women visiting outside the stall, washing hands and tediously applying lip gloss. Jill joins them at the washing basin.

"Hi, are you from Geneva?" Jill makes eye contact with the taller woman; she has kind eyes.

"Yes, you must be American." The woman smiles, and bats her long lashes. She's polite, but barely interested in Jill, and Jill wonders if she's being rude by interrupting the conversation taking place. She has to say something. The Swiss woman seems to be a shot at a connection. Someone who can help.

"Yeah, umm, my friend and I just came in on the train this evening from Paris. Actually, we were going to stay at the hostel down the street, but it's full. Now we're stuck and not sure what to do." Jill takes a step closer to the woman, confessing with total honesty the awful situation she's floundering in.

The tall, elegant woman pauses before answering. Studying Jill's eyes with compassion. She doesn't miss a beat. "Well, my advice to you, is to not worry about your lodging now and go play pool. Everything is so expensive in Switzerland, especially pool." She places a hand on Jill's shoulder and gives her a gentle pat. "Good luck to you."

The two women exit the bathroom, leaving Jill alone, and feeling even more stranded. She thinks to herself. "Ouch, if you can't even talk to someone sister to sister in the women's bathroom, how cold and hardened is the rest of the crowd in the bar?" Jill realizes, this is not a Zeeburg scenario, as badly as she wishes for it to be. No one here will offer any help to Mia and Jill. She can do nothing but take the bathroom woman's advice and go play pool.

With her head hung low, Jill joins Mia back at the table. Fortunately, Mia has had a mood change, and her enjoyment of the pool puts Jill at ease. They have each other, and, together, they can work things out.

"It's weird here." Mia whispers to Jill.

"I know. Do you want to get another beer?"

"Yeah, let's do that, after we finish our game. I mean, what else are we going to do. No place to go, babe."

Jill returns the balls and empty glasses. She purchases two more small beers, again holding her open palm of cash out to the bartender, thankful the woman looks honest. Jill and Mia carry their little beers to a small outside alcove that has built-in speakers. Jill smiles, discovering the source of the music they had heard from all the way downstairs in the train station. Mia and Jill watch several more people enter the bar, while others exit. A couple of people even join them outside to smoke their cigarettes in the fresh air. Nothing is really shared beyond a simple greeting with the Swiss pool players. While the beer recedes, and the glasses are nearly emptied, Mia and Jill feel their anxiety increase slightly.

Jill sighs. "Do you want to stay and have another drink?"

Mia shakes her head no.

"Do you want to leave?"

Mia shakes her head yes.

The women set their glasses down on a table and humbly walk out of the strange and inhospitable pool hall.

"Let's go down and hang out at the train station. It was nice there. We can sit and visit."

Jill's thankful, Mia's being a soldier about the situation. She's grateful Mia isn't demanding they go stay in the four hundred and fifty dollar hotel. Once back down on the lower level, next to the trains, they study the simple environment. The station is covered, and sort of indoors. It's big and open, with bright lights. There are vending machines with treats, and the place is completely empty.

"What time do you think it is?" Mia asks Jill.

"Look, it's half past midnight." Jill points to a big clock hanging above the station concessions.

"It's not bad here. It's bright, warm, and not too scary. Did you say our train to Zermatt leaves at six thirty tomorrow morning?" Mia waivers, doing her best to see the bright side of the situation.

Jill stares at a stationary train, shut down for the evening as she listens to Mia's thoughts. They huddle on a carpeted area against a wall. Setting their packs down, and sitting on top of them.

"So, we have six hours. I don't want to go get that expensive hotel room for six hours. That's a waste. I don't think I'd mind just hanging out here."

"Like, right here, in the train station?" Jill broke into the happiest feeling she'd had all night. "You know this is crazy, right? This is a real adventure. Mia, we're homeless in Switzerland. Vagrants, spending the night in a train station, all alone! This is so awesome! Yeah, we can definitely do it. Let's stay here!"

So, the two companions adopt a new program. This is a challenge, and after the boredom endured in the pool hall, camping in a foreign train station becomes the best fun. They hoist up there heavy packs, and move them over to a clear space beside the two vending machines which are stocked full of European confections. They push the packs up against the cold brick wall, then sit down on the floor and use the luggage for back rests. They can still hear the crappy rock music drifting downward and bouncing off the empty spaces in the station. For no precise reason, the two friends burst into a fit of laughter. Comfortable and no longer desperate, they find this new scene more than bizarre. The plan to wait out the night at the station, is almost too simple. The tiredness, and dulling from the beer, make their decision feel even more obscure.

Twenty minutes pass before they can't resist the urge to explore. They stand up to study the electric light within the vending machine. Jill tosses in some coins and purchases a candy bar. She breaks the chocolate in half, and passes a piece to Mia. They sit back down, and stare at the images painted across long-reaching advertisements plastered along the tunnels of the station. Most of them have scantily clad women in provocative poses.

One has an almost naked man, bulging out of his speedy swimsuit, pushing out his well-defined six pack abs. The women grin and slowly devour the chocolate.

Two trains are parked for the night. One train has lights on, and the other is dark. Almost an hour has passed, and Mia and Jill discover they're more at ease in the lonely station than they've been all day long. Comfortable, until they see two men walking towards them. They're older, perhaps in their late thirties or early forties. They have jackets and scarves on, and are laughing about something. Probably laughing at the sight of Mia and Jill, hunched down with their bags, staring vacantly at the parked trains.

"What should we do?" whispers Mia.

Jill creeps closer to her friend. "They're just on their way home. They'll be gone in a few minutes. We're okay."

"Jill, what if they're drunk? What if they want to hurt us? What if they're gypsies?"

Jill half wants to laugh, and half wants to cry. Mia's concerns are both silly and scary; because the truth could be lurking somewhere within her questions. Jill feels compelled to offer her companion a promise of security, but deep down, knows she can't honestly make that guarantee. Deep down, Jill is just as afraid as Mia.

The men walk straight over to the two women, and give them a warm smile. "Good evening, ladies. A little early to catch a train, huh?"

The two men start to laugh. The women squirm, trying to find a reasonable response. The man who spoke shoves his hand into his pocket, and Mia shifts herself forward, preparing to stand up. He pulls out some coins, which he smoothly drops into the vending machine slot. Mia eases back, but only a bit.

"We're supposed to stay at the hostel tonight, but they didn't have any rooms. We're stranded here for now." Jill concludes the truth is the only acceptable excuse to be sitting in a train station with huge packs after midnight. The man bends down, pulling his treat from the machines mouth. He stands back and unwraps the chocolate and hazelnut sweet. He keeps his eyes down on the chocolate, considering the information that Jill has shared.

"You don't have to be stranded. You can come home with us. I have a nice house, just a twenty minute drive from here."

"No, thanks, we just don't feel good about getting in a car with people we don't know. We just got here, I mean to Switzerland, a few hours ago. We've made the decision to stay right here. But, thank you." Mia responds, with no hesitation, revealing her strength and control over the situation.

Both men start laughing, looking very buzzed and amused. The man with the candy holds his hand out and offers a piece to each girl. Jill takes the candy, she works hard to conceal her fear.

"So, ladies, you don't have to ride with strangers. You can drive my car. Here are the keys." He laughs, while reaching into his pocket to jingle a set of keys. The jingle cuts through the big space of the train tunnel, and even drowns out the echo of the pool hall music for a second. Jill backs up, pressing herself into her pack, still clutching the small piece of hazelnut candy. For a moment, she imagines what would happen if they went with these two strange Euro-men. She pictures them driving away in a mysterious car, over the dark hills, further away from the center of town towards an unknown house. She shakes her mind free of the unwanted possibility.

"Thanks for the candy, but we're going to stay right here. We'll be okay," Mia assures the drunk men.

The men stand back, and take in the view of the two wayward travelers. They look at one another, communicating something with their eyes. Then they turn to Mia and Jill. The friendlier of the two, tips his brown plaid cap. Jill catches his eyes as they pass over her, they seem gentle and non-threatening. She second guesses if they should let the men help them.

Then, with nothing more to discuss, the men turn and continue to walk in the direction they were going. Jill and Mia remain stiff and focused, until the strangers are out of sight. Jill fingers the unusual chocolate and hazelnut treat, before taking a small bite. It's delicious. Mia eats hers, and the sobering encounter leaves both women silent for over fifteen minutes.

Jill swallows her last bite of the candy. "I was worried they would come back. I think they're pretty drunk. I'm pretty sure they won't be bothering us for the rest of the night."

"Yeah, I think they were nice . . . but, I'm glad they're gone. Jill, we shouldn't take candy from strangers!" The women giggle, huddled together, tucked into the corner of the enormous station. The big clock is now a quarter past two.

"Four and a half more hours. Should we sleep in shifts?" Jill suggests. Just then, the music from above cuts off. The stillness and shadows start to build and introduce new bothersome thoughts into their heads.

"I think we should both stay up. In case anything happens. Are you tired?" Mia asks, trying to empower herself during these lonesome hours of the night.

"I had that nap on the train today. I'm good." Jill answers.

For the next half an hour Mia and Jill are overcome with creativity and play. They take Jill's cameras out, and take dramatic pictures of themselves sprawled out on the train station floor, trying to look destitute. They snap a picture of a funny European man with a curly ponytail and spandex shorts who jogs past them sometime close to three in the morning.

"Oh, wow, these are going to be my favorite pictures of the whole trip. We now have evidence of: the night we were homeless in Switzerland. Hey Mia, look!"

A singular man, close in age to Jill and Mia is slowly making his way over to them. He's all alone, and has a subdued expression on his face. The women can't tell where he came from or figure why he's there.

Mia skips over to him, "Hi."

The young man grins bashfully, "Hi."

Mia laughs. "What's your name? Where did you come from? Do you want to sit with us?"

He's lean and tall, with wavy dark brown hair and quiet blue eyes. He has an orange shirt on, with a kaki jacket covering half his body, a black wool scarf is wrapped tightly around his neck. "I'm Cedric. I work on the trains. I am from France. Yes, I would like to sit with you."

His answers make Mia delight in the odd ghost of a boy who might just be the only other living thing around the train station at this hour.

"Hi, I'm Cedric." He respectfully introduces himself once more to Jill. He's just as awake and sober as the women, and why he is there; doesn't even matter. Its heaven sent to have a distraction to ease their time, and bring them closer to morning. Jill blushes, she can't decide if he's handsome or not.

"You work on the trains?" Mia asks as the trio settle back down to the floor, near their packs.

"Yes, I clean the trains at night. Sometimes I work here, but other times I might be in different places."

The women listen intently, imagining what it must be like to be up all night, working on trains all alone.

"You do this work on your own, Cedric?" Jill asks.

"I have a boss. He'll be here at six. I can introduce you to him if you like." Then he looks around, pausing to think. "I have a room back over that way. You can put your things in it. I can lock everything up if you need. It's a good place." Cedric's English is limited, but he works hard to explain himself, and the women find his ability to interpret sweet.

Still, a good room sounds questionable. It's suspicious that he wants to take them off somewhere unknown. At three in the morning, no one should be trusted, not even tame singular men. Jill and Mia exchange glances. They both tire from being so defensive all evening. They decide to submit to curiosity and the desire for a better refuge. They put their faith in the random train cleaner and go to see his room.

The women stand up, then Cedric. They go to lift their packs, but Cedric stands in front of them; waving his hand.

"No, I will carry these for you." Cedric is goofy but nice. They don't have to follow him far before they reach a spot along the wall where a small unmarked door extends out with a partition. They watch him pull a key out of his pocket and unlock the practically invisible door. It opens wide, and he holds it until Jill and Mia pass through. He flicks a switch and the room flashes in fluorescent light. Mia and Jill remain where they stand, waiting for their eyes to adjust to the brightness within. The room has a counter with a sink and cabinets fastened above. Beside the counter is a refrigerator and a microwave. A couch is pushed up against one wall, and in the middle of the room floats a break table, complete with napkin dispenser placed neatly in the center. Cedric unloads the two packs on the couch. The girls pull up a chair at the table. They're impressed that this "surprise visitor" has lead them to such a warm and safe shelter. This new scenario amplifies the contradiction between the insecure qualities of the train station, and the idea that this place is their lodging for the night.

"Okay, Jill and Mia," he pauses to give each woman a meaningful smile. "Would you like some hot chocolate or hot tea?" He folds his hands together, politely waiting on his guest's request.

Mia answers first. "Do you have peppermint tea?"

"No, I am sorry, Mia. I have Lipton's tea." He holds out a yellow and red packet.

"Okay." Mia smiles graciously.

"Jill, what would you like?"

Jill appreciates the way Cedric perfectly divides his attention between herself and Mia. "Lipton's sounds great."

"I'll have tea, too," he announces warmly, while turning to prepare their late night drink.

Under the sharp florescence, Jill and Mia watch Cedric microwave some water, then add the steaming liquid to three short Styrofoam cups. He distributes the cups, and passes out the tea bags wrapped individually in crisp yellow paper. Silence spills through the room, and the women sit amused, watching him fix the tea. Mia catches Jill's glance, and they both erupt into laughter. Laughing because they are now sitting in a Swiss train station break room with a French man, and laughing because it's sometime around three in the morning, and laughing because now they are drinking tea. Cedric starts to laugh, too. The humor of the situation hasn't escaped him, and he's grateful to have such interesting company during the loneliest hours of his shift.

"Are we keeping you, Cedric, do you have to get back to work soon?" Jill asks affectionately.

Cedric pulls out a chair, and joins the women around the common oval table. "No, I'm fine. I can stay with you both as long as you need me. I am on a break."

"I know, Cedric, but if you have work to do," Mia stops to rethink her suggestion. "I know, we could help you clean the trains!" Mia coaxes, wanting to repay Cedric for his kindness.

Jill nods, inspired by Mia's noble idea.

When a stranger reaches out and gives, or performs a good deed, it has a special way of affecting one's spirit. This affect is exponentially more during the coldest and latest hours of the night. The possibility of being useful and helpful, brightens the stale early morning atmosphere.

Cedric laughs in a bashful way. "It's so nice of you, but really, I'm okay. I will sit and drink tea with you. Don't worry about my work. It's stupid work, anyway."

The women grow quiet, realizing that Cedric feels obliged to sort of "rescue" them. He is doing his best to be their hero. In a way, he pretty much is a hero. Mia and Jill study this new character. He's thin, with tired eyes that have been up working all night. He isn't handsome by traditional standards, but he has an attractive quality about him that puts both women at ease. Tall, with pale extra-large eyes that give him features that remind Jill of some sort of nocturnal night creature from the nature documentaries she loves to watch back home. This makes her wonder if he looks this way from too many nights working alone cleaning trains. Did he physically morph and adapt to his lifestyle, like the birds of Galapagos? Or was he genetically predisposed to find work that requires him to lurk around vacant train depots in the dead of night? And if he is, what does this say about Jill? What would Jill's genetically predisposed vocation be? What are short, chunky, white women with big hips and a big nose intended to do? Her mind pulls her to unusual places, during these peculiar hours of night.

"Why did you travel to Switzerland from America?" Cedric asks, looking genuinely fascinated by the women. Even though he works on trains and the train system, he acts like he's never seen travelers before.

Mia and Jill look at one another and try to create a simplified reason. They stop to let the steam from their cups curl under their noses, arousing exhausted senses.

"I'm not sure. We are . . . just on a vacation. We wanted to see Europe, and I really want to see Zermatt and the Matterhorn," Jill responds, trying to make the explanation easy to relate to. "Have you ever wanted to visit the United States?" Jill inquires, feeling thankful to have someone to make small talk with over a nice cup of tea, versus sitting on the cold ground in a foreign train station.

"No, I never really thought about going to the United States." Cedric can tell from their expression, that they're surprised by his answer. He smiles, and laughs. "Does everybody in the U.S think that everyone else in the world wants to go to their country?" The forward comment, embarrasses the women.

Jill looks across the table at Mia. Even though she looks revived and perky after a few sips of Lipton's, she still appears to have the "homeless persona" that she assumed earlier in the night. Fighting fatigue and the chill in the air is more than she can tolerate. Jill can see its taking a toll.

Jill wants a fair assessment of how Cedric might judge them, so she looks at her friend, pretending it's for the first time. There sits a sleepless, homeless woman, with the back of her short hair frizzed straight up, and the front smoothed straight back. Earlier in the night, Mia had given herself a forehead massage to calm her tired nerves. She massaged the front of her scalp, which gave her hair its own signature style. Her sweater compliments the hair, because it's been triple layered, which makes her head look extra small. But the thing that really adds to the "small head syndrome" is the fact that Mia has wrapped her oatmeal brown scarf around her neck at least four times. Jill thinks, "*If a magic fairy had been flying through some enchanted wood, and offered to turn a turtle into a human, the result would look a lot like Mia this evening.*" Jill decides to enjoy her friend's unkempt look, since the entire trip she's looked nothing less than amazing. Jill takes a long look at her friend, encouraged by the fact that tonight; she is the better dressed. "

All of the sudden, Mia starts to unwrap the scarf from her throat. Jill inches back in her chair, disturbed at the possibility her friend somehow knew she was thinking rotten thoughts. Mia raises her hands to her head, and smooths down the rest of her hair style. This makes Jill extra paranoid. Thoughts jumble in her tired brain. "*She must have seen me looking at her hair and scarf!*"

Jill thinks about herself, and how she might appear from Cedric's point of view. Halfway through the night Jill had swapped her sweatshirt for a black pullover sweater. She's in jeans, and her shoes with the built-in pockets that are multi-colored with hues that do not exist in nature. She has her travel pocket tucked under the sweater, and both the cameras securely resting against her chest. Her own hair has been swept up and twisted into a floppy bun on the top of her head. She's sure her makeup wore off hours ago, and imagines her face looks washed out and pale. "Cedric is right, why would we even entertain the thought that people in other countries might want to visit a region where ultra-weirdos, such as myself come from?"

She starts to understand how repellent they might be. Then Jill imagines the two of them together. Two American half-wits, riding by the seat of their pants, through countries they could barely order a meal in, congratulating themselves on how great they were because they came from the United States, and missing the whole point of why they came. These disturbing thoughts are interrupted by Mia, who's thankfully taking charge and salvaging what's left of the early morning.

"So, Cedric, you clean the trains at night. Do you like your job?" Mia asks, while taking an inventory of the details of the generic break room.

"Yes, it is okay. It is just a job. I don't mind the work." He gives her a warm smile, that makes Mia recognize his culture and personal values are different from hers, and she accepts that it's wrong to assume he regards the same things she does, with misplaced importance.

"And what do you both do for work?"

Jill beams with nostalgia to tell him about their job. She knows he wouldn't quite understand, no matter how hard she explains. This is probably due to the fact that they hardly do anything at their job. "We work at a children's museum in California."

"Aaah, a museum. We have many of these around France. You like art?"

"Well, yes, but we don't have art or historical stuff, it's a Children's Museum." Jill tries to persuade him to think more on the subject.

"So, it's about children? People go there to look at children? Here, sometimes people do that at parks, but they can get arrested." Cedric scratches his head, squinting his eyes, suspecting the train women might try to fool him.

The women purr with giggles.

Jill's tempted to let him think that in America, there are museums that feature children on display for public exhibition. But, she can see he's beginning to lose his sense of humor.

"It's a museum for kids. Instead of art on the walls, we might put out paint and paper on a table. Instead of sculptures, we have a water cycle structure that they can climb. Our job is to make sure the kids visiting the Museum aren't running, or breaking exhibits."

"We're the fun police," adds Mia, winking at Jill.

Jill nods, and takes a third sip of her tempered black tea.

"Oh, okay. I understand." Cedric offers, uninterested in the idea of an anti-museum with no art or culture, where kids run around crazy.

Mia decides she wants to change the subject. "So, Cedric, what is there to see around here?

"See around here?"

"Yeah, we've never been to Geneva. Are their special things we should try to see, other than the pool hall with the terrible music upstairs?"

Cedric laughs again, and seems to share their dislike for the pool hall. "Well, have you seen the lake?"

"Sort of, we saw a part of it when we passed by on the train. I would love to see the lake."

"Okay." Cedric stands up, and sets down his cup.

Mia and Jill just sit silent, wondering what he is going to do. He just stares back at them, smiling sweetly.

Mia, gets the connection before Jill. "Now?"

"Yes, why not? I'll take you to see the lake now." Cedric folds his arms across his chest, waiting for the women to rise from their metal folding chairs. "Here, leave your packs in the room. I'll lock everything up safe."

Blindly trusting the three am stranger; the girls say goodbye to all the belongings they have, minus Jill's traveler's pouch, which she double wound around her neck. They follow Cedric down a corridor and out into the chilled night air. The road is illuminated by street lights and shop signs.

"Come on Mia, come on Jill, this way." He gently coaxes.

Like leaping off a cliff into the depths of a river basin, Jill and Mia step out from the station aware of the risk. Mia feels a small surge of adrenaline hit her the same time the cool lake air does. It's just past four in the morning, and the odd man has a fast pace that Mia and Jill find a struggle to keep up with. He doesn't slow down for them. Down to the end of a street that dead ends, they make a fast right and continue on to another street, then another immediate right down a darker narrow passage that leads to apartments. Fifteen minutes pass, and they are still walking, deeper into Switzerland and further from the security of the station. The streets are completely still, they see no people, nor cars during the walk.

Cedric breaks to a clean stop. "There". He points to the dark black void just beyond a row of trees.

Jill looks hard, she squints trying to make her wired eyes focus on the water. Within seconds she can make out the reflection of stars waving on the surface of the immense lake. Cedric starts to move again, and the women work hard to stay right behind him, fearing the possibility of getting lost. Soon they find themselves at the entrance to a small park. There's a sand box, a jungle gym, and a swing set. The three night creepers help themselves to a swing, sitting so they face the lake. Now Jill can see a little more. She sees the lights of boats on the opposite shoreline, and another city, sparkling and towering miles across the water.

Being so dark; less looking takes place, more listening happens. All three are silent as they watch and use their ears to decipher what their eyes cannot. The noises down by the lakes edge sound like a swift and coarse poem, sensorial, reminding each of the solidarity of existing in this place, at this time. Straddling the point in the earth, where the lake and the land meet; they ponder thoughts that might be shared, but won't be discussed. Chatter and conversation are for those who frequent normal hours. For those who are together, outside for nothing specific, at four in the morning, words are unnecessary. The place, the sound of the mild waves lapping against rocks, an early songbird warming up before the sun rises, a discussion between crickets, are all that can be heard. They are all that need to be heard. The stress and fear from the long night falls away, and all that remains is a calm and vast alpine lake.

Cedric ends the moment, fishing for gratitude, or a little understanding. "Okay, girls, here is the lake, do you like it?"

"It's beautiful, Cedric, thank you for taking us here," Jill whispers, drowning in the spell of an enchanting night in a Swiss dream. The trio plays on the playground, and even moves down closer to the water's edge. With morning looming in the near future, Jill, Mia, and Cedric begin walking back to the station a little slower.

When they arrive at the station, language games are a welcome distraction to pass the final hour with Cedric. Mia points at a poster plastered to the station wall. The poster reads something in Swiss and has glistening, toned legs and butts in bikini bottoms. The tops of the women are cut off so only their legs and asses are showcased.

"What do you call this?" Mia points at the butts.

"?Fessée," Cedric answers with finesse.

"Fess?" The women repeat the word back several times.

"Fessée," Cedric says with validation, admiring the row of Swiss ass.

The sun is rising, people start to show up. Slowly the bustle of the train station expands with activity. The café opens up, and early morning commuters are shuffling in and out to purchase coffee and croissant. The ticket booth opens, so Mia and Jill grab their tickets to Zermatt.

"Wow, Jill, they're eighty extra dollars in addition to our four hundred dollar Eurail pass."

"I'm positive Zermatt will be completely worth it. Just focus on the prize. Mia, it's the Matterhorn!" Jill begs, she's in no mood for complaints this morning.

Mia warms up to Jill's enthusiasm. She's curious why her companion harbors such a passion for the Swiss Alps.

Cedric is waiting near a bench in front of the ticket office, he waves to someone just beyond a line of people waiting to buy reading material at a magazine stand.

"Jill, Mia, I want you to meet someone. This is my boss." Cedric scurries off, disappearing for a second, hidden within the waves of commuters. He emerges with an older gray-haired man wearing a flannel jacket. The man looks curious, following Cedric over to Mia and Jill. The women patiently listen to the two men speak back and forth several times in French. Then the man extends his hand to introduce himself.

"Hi, my name is Jean. Cedric tells me you were stuck at the station last night without a room to stay. I'm so glad you ran into Cedric. He's very fond of you both."

Mia and Jill step forward to meet Cedric's boss. He's very laid back and eager to help, the same way Cedric is.

Cedric takes Jill's arm and sweetly informs her, "Jean would like to buy you both breakfast. Come with us."

With shy smiles, the women follow the two train station men toward the café with the glass panels all around. Jean jumps into the crowded line, yelling something to Cedric.

Cedric turns to Mia. "He wants to know if you want one or two pastry?" Jill and Mia exchange a puzzled look.

"Jill, should we share one?"

"Oh, yeah, of course." Jill agrees.

Mia turns to Cedric. "We'll take one to share."

Cedric starts to laugh from his gut, his brown eyes crinkle at the ends in delight. "No, one or two a piece!"

"Oh, we would like one a piece then." Mia's face turns red, and she wonders if the man is trying to feed them because he thinks they're homeless and maybe would need a second croissant for lunch or something.

They both watch Cedric shout something else in French and hold up a finger to make a sign for "one". The digital schedule on the big sign, declares that the train to Zermatt will be leaving in twenty minutes and that passengers can board in five minutes. Jean walks over with a drink carrier with four stiff coffees and two bags of treats.

He holds out the coffees for Mia and Jill to help themselves. They're both grateful for the hot caffeinated drinks, and for a moment Jean gives them a look that's richer and warmer than the coffee. His kindness distracts Mia and Jill from their very good, and very new friend, Cedric. Jean is really affectionate with Cedric too. It makes Jill wonder if they might be father and son.

"Well, let's get your bags, girls." Cedric speaks softly while clutching his paper coffee cup. They follow him back to the break room, but this time they wait outside. Cedric enters alone, and pulls out their bags. He helps each woman with the technical straps. Then he passes a paper bag to Mia.

"Pan au chocolates. You'll love them."

The bag is heavy, and, in spots, translucent from the butter seeping out of the pastry. He follows Mia and Jill to their train. They turn to say goodbye. This farewell is more challenging than they'd prepared for. Jill wonders, "How do you say thank you to someone for a break room, or tea, a late night lake walk, or pan au chocolate?"

But, more than all of that, it was his kindness and the mysterious way he came to their rescue when they needed the help so desperately."

They face Cedric, he looks touched by the moment as well. In a strange mutual sort of connection, the trio exchanges hugs and words of thanks before breaking free, taking their separate paths.

As the train rolls away from the station, Jill's attention is redirected to the greasy sweet bag of pastry. She doesn't give Cedric another thought.

Sept

Jill and Mia finish every bite of the hearty breakfast confection. They sip the final gulps of their fresh Swiss coffee. The train moves, climbing and twisting past expressive mountain passes that have a way of telling stories of time and spirit. The wildflowers are in bloom, and Jill appreciates being able to just watch out the window at the confetti of colors sprinkled across high meadows of grass. Other than the occasional cow, or a tree, the scenery is open and cultivates a desire to explore. Jill leans back and decides to copy Mia, who is now catching a quick cat nap before they reach the next train stop.

Jill wakes to a puddle of drool on her own shoulder, and a familiar hand on her arm, nudging her back into consciousness. "Jill, we have to get off here."

"Where?" Jill asks, looking around to process another new place in the world. The train is on the top of a high pointed mountain. The tracks just end, and to the left is a little shelter, without a soul in sight.

"Here, come on. Our ticket says we have to get off here, and wait for our train."

"Oh, yeah, I remember. But seriously, here?" Jill hesitates, she sees the doubt that hangs from her companion's face.

"I know, this is creepy, and I'm not even sure, but I think we need to get off here. Like, right now, this train is leaving!"

Jill and Mia tug and pull their burdensome packs off the train, and toss them in a pile on a boardwalk. They stand, staring at the train, it lets out a whistle, then reverses itself back the way it had come.

Jill starts to laugh hysterically. "Look at this! What the hell? We're in the middle of nowhere on top of a mountain!"

The mountain is steep, and they can see out to grand empty valleys below them. The valleys are held by other empty high peaks. The women turn to explore the small train shelter. There's an indoor area and a ticket booth. Both of these features are shut down, and no one else is anywhere in sight. A vending machine that's nestled along the boardwalk is the only sign that they're in some sort of remote version of civilization.

"Whoa, this is crazy. Look, we're all alone, accept for those mountain goats over there. So, another train is going to pull up, and we get on that one?" Jill asks, questioning their security and direction in the country.

"Yeah, the ticket doesn't say when the train comes, but it says we have to take it, if we want to get to Zermatt."

"So, how will we know which train is the right train to get on?"

Mia looks irritated, and with her best effort to cooperate and support Jill, responds dryly, "You, my friend, are going to ask the conductor. That's how we'll know. This was your thing, remember? Coming up here to the middle of who- knows -where."

Jill can't deny Mia's point, and can only hope that the train will show up and take them to Zermatt very soon. "Hey, look on the bright side, we have hostel reservations waiting for us. Real beds to sleep in tonight, and showers."

The thought of reservations comforts Mia. They try to relax and enjoy the views from the top of the nameless alpine peak.

. . . . .

Two hours pass, finally a train shows up. Mia finds a passenger who can assure them that the train is bound for Zermatt. Soon the travelers are rolling again. The train pulls them higher and deeper into the Swiss Alps. Even though the views are epic, after turning around the hundredth bend and twist, the women grow restless.

Eventually a modernized train station gleams in the snow-capped distance. Jill's heart starts to beat fast. They made it! Only weeks ago, it was her wildest dream to see Zermatt, and now here she is, sitting with anticipation as the train carries her closer to the ideal. She scoots up to the edge of her seat, and wiggles her toes that are pinched in her special neon green travel shoes with the secret pockets on the sides. "Mia, we're here. Can you believe it? We made it. How we figured it all out, I don't know, but, we made it!" Jill starts to tremble with excitement.

. The train roars into the station, and stops with stealth. Mia and Jill collect their things. They shuffle off the train with two other passengers. Within minutes, the train is gone.

"I'm happy to be done with trains for a few days. But, uh, where are we exactly?" Mia makes a half circle in place, trying to get her bearings and review the town. She sees the other passengers quickly moving down a corridor, and down a road. "Hmmm, let's follow them."

They steady the packs, balancing them with their hips, following the short trail that the older man and woman had used. When they finally reach the town, it's painfully obvious. If one closed their eyes and imagined a typical Swiss Alpine Ski Town, Zermatt would probably enter into the mind. Swiss Chalet's with rustic wood trim around the windows tower along a narrow main street. Flags are hung outside shops, and strewn across passageways. At first Jill wonders if they were in some sort of shopping square, but after walking for some time, she decides that this cheerfully decorated street, is in fact, the town of Zermatt. Jill speaks to herself in her mind. She slowly utters "Zermatt", letting the z sound roll from her tongue like a confessed secret. More steps take them further into town. Mia and Jill notice that there are hardly any people around, and many of the shops are closed. They must have planned a visit in between ski season, and the summer mountaineering season. Jill feels a little disappointed that she's missed the tourist season. She's been hoping to meet some fellow travelers with a fondness for alpine adventure.

"I'm so hungry, Jill. Let's find a place to eat."

"Food sounds perfect. We'll eat, then find our hostel," Jill replies.

They scan the village, and all the café's appear closed. "Oh, thank God, look, a McDonalds." Jill grabs Mia's hand and starts to pull her towards the big familiar golden arches.

"Oh, what? But, we can get that crappy food back in the states."

Jill isn't listening to Mia. She has her eyes and stomach fixated on the greasy fried symbol of home. "Mia, it's cheap, it will fill us up, and I'm not sure where else to go to find food right now."

Two quarter-pounders with cheese and two large fries later, the women emerge from the commercialized institution, full and heavy from carbs. Again, they find themselves wandering down the main street, gawking at the shop windows and apartments above the street.

"Our map shows that we have to go all the way to the end of this street, then we'll find a road that kind of dead ends. We want to follow the road for about a half a mile, our hostel should be to the right. Help me look for the sign. It should say Matterhorn Hostel out front." Jill instructs, wanting so badly to guide her traveling partner to their destination with ease.

Jill's been pretty demanding of Mia over the last couple days, and she's patiently endured more than any friend should be expected to. This is clearly Jill's wish to visit Zermatt, and she wants more than anything to make the experience as painless as possible for Mia. Jill reasons that if she works hard enough, she can create a fantastic experience for her friend.

Three ski bum-esque looking men pass Jill and Mia; walking in the opposite direction. They catch Jill's eye, and she thinks they could be the key to finding a fun night life in the sleepy little town. They have tie dye shirts and blonde dreadlocks.

"Hey, fine ladies!" The taller guy in the middle calls out. "Welcome to Zermatt!" He greets them, eying their backpacks.

They don't slow down, and Jill barely has a chance to wave back at them before they vanish out of sight. Mia rolls her eyes at the dorky hippie men. Since they left the Zeeburg campground back in Amsterdam, her most persistent wish is to return and spend some time with their fun-natured new friends.

When the women come to an intersection to turn right, they catch their first glimpse of the mountain.

"Oh, my, God," gasps Mia.

"There it is," whispers Jill. "No, no, just wait. Let's stop right here." Jill stammers, before sliding her pack off of her shoulders, letting it drop with a thud to the ground.

"Good thing you didn't pack anything fragile in there," Mia says.

"Nope, I've got my cameras right here. Come on, stand right here by this rock. I'll take your picture with the Matterhorn in the background."

Mia walks over to the rock, and as she poses for her portrait, Jill can see through her viewfinder that her friend is happy, affected by the gnarled, glaciated, precipice of one's dream. She steadies her camera and watches her friend for a few seconds through the lens. She wants to capture her, and the way she's feeling here in this mysterious little niche of geology.

Jill passes her camera's off to Mia so she can make her own poses to mark the discovery and arrival that was, until now, only a fantasy.

After pictures, they remain in the middle of the street, packs laying in chaos, while they stand mesmerized by the shape and movement of the pressurized ice and rock. The sun is shining just behind the slim, tall mountain. Most of the peak is covered in snow, and a few ski lifts are operating, despite the lack of skiers.

Soon, packs are picked up, and re-secured to bodies. Once again, the weary travelers summon the gusto to keep moving down the new path. The road opens up, while buildings spread apart. A babbling creek, and glacial erratics add to the Swiss experience. Soon, they see an old weathered two-story building sitting off to the right.

"There it is!" Mia cheers.

Once inside the hostel, a pleasant Swiss man takes them through a small passage toward the back of the building. They timidly make their way down a miniature flight of stairs, before swinging a sharp left to a hall that offers three small rooms. At the end of the hall is a restroom with several showers that are divided by faded shower curtains.

"So ladies, this will be your room. The older Swiss man walks into the room with them. They see two sets of bunk beds, and two small twin beds situated across a narrow space. There is only one small window near the top of the back wall. Sun is shining in, and making a gold rectangle on the middle of the wooden floorboards.

"You can pick any of the beds you like. There are two men who are staying here, also. They seem very nice." He points to a bunk that has a pile of luggage, and some climbing ropes scattered across it. "Enjoy your stay, dears." The hostel host leaves the women to unpack and freshen up.

Mia flops down on the twin bed that rests closest to her. "So, two matters of business we need to discuss. One, we made it! That's amazing. How did we even find this place? We did a good job. I can't believe last night we were homeless with no place to go. Two, did he say, there are two nice men that are going to be sleeping with us tonight in this little room?" When Mia spoke of the second issue, her voice waivers with concern and doubt.

Jill sits down on the bed beside Mia. "Yeah, look, they have ropes. They must be mountain climbers. Maybe they'll be hot."

Mia sits up and gives her friend an urgent look. Okay, they could be mountain climbers, but what if they have those ropes to tie up dumb American girls who think they can just show up at a random hostel in the middle of nowhere?"

Jill's silent, trying to digest the new twist in their journey. Admiring her companion's discerning ways. "No way, they won't be weird. They'll probably be really fun, and cute, like our guys in Amsterdam."

Jill shifts back. "But, I did see a gift shop full of Swiss pocket knives. I guess it won't hurt to pick one up. Then if we get tied up, we'll have something to cut the ropes with." She lets out a sinister laugh.

Mia grabs a stale scented pillow and throws it as hard as she can at Jill, smirking as she aims. "So, which beds should we take?" Mia prompts Jill to devise a plan now, instead of later. A plan is the best they can do for the time being.

"We can share the other bunk bed. That way we'll stay together, in case others show up tonight."

"Oh wow, that's true. We could get more people in this little room." Mia says.

"Shower?"

"For sure."

Soon hot water pours over the tired and sweaty women. Hot water on sore feet, hot water over tired eye lids, hot water on tight knotted necks, and hot water through oily curls of hair. All the time spent together, facing challenges, and even showering together, separated by a cheap vinyl curtain. Curtain or not, the compression of togetherness is starting to put stress on the relationship.

Even though it's only four thirty, the friends decide to eat trail mix from their packs and go to bed. Jet-lag and running around Geneva at all hours, have them ready to surrender the day, and let sleep repair the stress that's built up. Sometime after ten, they're lightly woken by the sound of men moving about in the dark of the room. Soft whispers, a few zippers opening access to packs, and the room is silent.

.　　　.　　　.　　　.　　　.

Morning grabs Jill by surprise, with a sudden jolt of consciousness, she leans up and rolls out of the spring meshed bunk bed. She sits on the bare floor of the room, looking around. She remembers hearing the men last night, and had somehow left a post-it note in her mind, to register this information in the morning, when it might be more useful. The men are gone, and so are their things. The mattresses are empty, and give away no sign that the men were ever there. Perplexed, Jill pushes her arms back to raise herself to her feet. Her muscles stiffen, opposing the prospect of more traveling. Mia's been awoken by the swift thud Jill made when she hit the floor. She's leaning back in her bed, propped up by her forearms.

"Good morning."

She scratches her clean shampooed hair and moves down in her sleeping bag. "The men, I heard them last night." She stares at the four empty beds. "Are they gone?"

"Weird, huh? We didn't even get to meet them. I bet they're climbing the Matterhorn today, and had to get up at like four in the morning or something!" Jill explains enthusiastically, proud that she's able to interpret the function of this new culture. Mountain life she understands. Jill loves to watch documentaries about winter sports, and outdoor adventure. She reads books on the subject, and when the stars line up just right, she plans her own outdoor fun back home in California. Mia lays back down, flattening herself into the mattress. She stares up at the wood panels on the ceiling, contemplating the day.

"Showers, then breakfast?"

"It's a plan," Jill answers with zest. "After breakfast, we can go for a hike, or check out the shops. I want to see that cemetery we passed in town."

"Okay, Jill, we'll figure it all out. Did you see that bakery we walked past yesterday, with the cheese-filled horns? I bet they have incredible coffee."

"Oooh, I'm starving. Thinking about that place makes me want to skip the shower. I'll even skip getting dressed. Let's just walk down there in our pajamas. Now I understand why Cedric's boss asked if we wanted two pan au chocolate's each. Today, I could eat three."

Thinking of the kind old man, who wanted to buy them so many goodies, motivates the women to start the day with encouragement. Sometimes life has a way of happening, and if you just relax and let it, things have a way of working themselves out. This seems to be the method of traveling for the women. They roll with the sway of the world, and the trains, and the season. Cultures are merging and crashing up against the others as they intercept different geographies. Regardless of where they are, they are always Jill, and they are always, Mia. Nothing can change this, and knowing that, gives them peace.

It takes the women close to thirty minutes to walk to the bakery. The lights are on, and the display cases are over-flowing with different types of sugared temptations. It's a struggle to pick which treat to experience. Croissants with fruit compote; horns filled with sweet cheese, tarts, and muffins topped with toasted almonds, all invite a different memory and flavor. The food evokes so many emotions, the women stand hungry, in awe of the colorful assortment of breakfast fare.

"Two café au laits please." Mia isn't sure what a café au lait is, which is all the more reason to order one this morning. A poised Swiss woman in her late thirties nods and gives Jill and Mia a moment to decide on a pastry. Finally Jill selects a cream horn, and Mia picks something that looks like an éclair with some sort of nut mixture stuffed inside. After their divine Swiss breakfast, they wander over to a graveyard that sits opposite a striking and unusual Catholic church.

"Look at the architecture of that cathedral, Mia!"

Mia looks over and can see the same familiar obsessive glare Jill had back at Notre Dame. She rolls her eyes at the thought of having to spend the next two hours walking around a dark dusty church, when they're surrounded by some of the best natural habitat in the world.

"Mia, look, they have the times of the mass posted on this sign. I'm going to go to mass!" Jill announces with a hint of inspiration in her voice. "Come on, Mia, will you go to mass?"

Mia sighs, "How about this? I'll hang out in the graveyard with you and check out the cool headstones and that river, but then I think I'll head back to our room to get some down time. It will be nice to be by myself for a little while." Mia doesn't know how else to say it, and she knows it must sound a little rude.

Jill listens, considering, she shakes her head in understanding. "I think I'd love to have a little time by myself, too. I'm glad you said that, Mia. Let's go check out some graves, then."

Both Mia and Jill spark a fresh affection for the other, now that they've designed some time to separate. Even their body language loosens, and the good plan rejuvenates their perspective on the day.

The town looks empty. Jill keeps a look out for the colorful hippie guys from yesterday, but no one's around. It feels like the whole town has been abandoned. If it weren't for a few shop keepers lurking inside the stores, peering out from dark voids occasionally, Jill would suspect the whole town had been shut down. Now that they're in a graveyard, the tone becomes even creepier. The women push open the creaky metal gate and follow a little trail that twists around headstones and down a mellow grade, which recedes to a roaring river.

"Oh, look! This must be a graveyard for the mountain climbers," Jill whispers.

Mia focuses on Jill's remark, and realizes that the names on the headstones are of different origins, some sound like French names, others might have been from Russia, or the Czech Republic. The dates also reveal the departed all died relatively young. On some of the headstones, hiking boots had been placed, or ski poles poked out of the ground. She looks around at the final statements the climbers have made. Then, she looks up behind her at the great mountain towering just above. She recalls the night before, and reconsiders their ability to preserve themselves when they are so unsure of their environment. If they misread their own mountain on this personal expedition through Europe, would it lead to an untimely fate? Mia rolls her shoulders forward, and decides she's had enough of her morbid thoughts.

"Okay then, I'm going to take a nice walk back to the hostel and take a nap. I'll see you after church." With a single nod, she turns and respectfully walks back up the winding path, back through the creaking graveyard gate.

Jill remains where Mia's left her, close to the water's edge. She feels the relief of being alone. Every place Jill had been, and every decision that had been made, had to involve some sort of agreement or compromise. Now, she's alone, she's free to make her own choices independently. But, it wasn't just the concentration of friendship that had been distracting, it was, also, the traveling and interpreting of languages and directions. Here in the graveyard, by the swift Zermatt river, she can embrace the reason for which she came: to make discoveries. Discoveries about herself, and discoveries about the world, which are more than enticing, they are crucial. Unlike Mia, Jill's not an efficient or organized person. She moves a little slower, and needs to take things in on a more thoughtful level. She wants to pause, and take her time looking at the water flowing. She likes to memorize the way the ground tilts beneath her in the sacred cemetery. She wants to understand the odd language printed on the church sign, and pray in a more universal fashion, so that maybe God would smile for her.

. She looks up the embankment and can see a handful of people enter into the mysterious Chapel. She decides to watch a little longer, before she joins them. A chorus of bells starts to chime at St. Mauritius. Jill jolts from her firmly planted position in the empty stone garden. She quickly scuttles past the headstones, out through the little gate, straight across the street, and into the high alpine church, that for some reason, Jill finds irresistible.

As she passes through the heavy wooden doors, she immediately slows down her pace. She calmly walks to a middle area, dropping her knee, she lowers her head and makes the sign of the Trinity before finding a seat in a simple wooden pew. Finally, she allows herself to examine the intriguing temple. The square footage of the structure is conservative, but the high arched ceilings make up for the modest size. Jill appreciates how some of the spaces in the church are left plain, and then in corners, and near the ceiling, detailed pieces featuring saints and angels provoke strange thoughts and anxiety. Up toward the front is a prolific looking altar, and a perfect crucifix suspends from above. Jill can count those in attendance on her fingers. There are only nine other people anticipating the afternoon mass. Soon, altar boys enter, then the priest, and a tiny woman with a scarf over her head who plays the organ. When mass starts, Jill's delighted to find herself participating in a Latin mass for the first time. The service passes quickly and soon she's lined up in a small procession to receive the Holy Eucharist. Grateful for the gift, she returns to her post on the pew, kneeling down to pray and think. She contemplates her journey. The bells ring again, and Jill is on her way, sashaying back to the hostel with a skip in her step. She can't help it. The time was much needed. She is happy within herself.

Back at the hostel, Jill takes a place in a bed near Mia's. "How was church?" Mia asks sweetly.

"It was so perfect, Mia. You would have loved it."

"Yeah, I'm kind of regretting not going with you, but I was really tired. I feel so much better just taking some time for myself."

"I get that completely," Jill answers, her tone still vital and renewed.

The women hear the heavy voice of the hostel owner giving someone the introductory talk about showers, and meals, and things. Jill and Mia sit up in bed, alert, wondering who the new travelers might be. Then they hear female voices, foreign female voices. Disturbed by the intrusion, Jill and Mia sit, glaring at each other, wondering who they're about to meet. Seconds later, the nice old man leads two young Asian women into the room. "This is where you will be staying, with these two." He scratches his head looking around the room, instead of at Mia or Jill. The women are now sitting erect, preparing to greet their roommates.

"Hi, I'm Mia, this is my friend Jill."

"Hello, good day? I am fine. My name is Yang Sun. Name is Kai Chu." The Chinese woman replies enthusiastically. She's dressed in a modern traveling outfit.

Jill and Mia beam with smiles in response to the upbeat new roommates.

"So, I'll leave you to your room now. Ladies, if any of you need anything . . . I'm just upstairs, okay?" The hostel owner waves, then turns the corner.

The four women remain still, listening to the steady footsteps climb back up the unfinished wooden steps. When the footsteps fade, the conversation picks up.

"So, are you two traveling alone?" Mia asks.

"Yes, my parents were with me for part of way. I separate from them back in Amsterdam." Yang Sun answers in a sweet, passive tone.

"What? No way! We were just in Amsterdam, too!" Jill shares, happy to have something in common. The two girls take two empty beds. The tiny dark downstairs hostel room is somehow transformed into a cozy slumber party atmosphere.

All four females engage, scooting down to the ends of their beds. Today, all four have claimed a lower bunk, ground level bed.

Jill decides to reach out and take part in the socialization. Two traveling women, meet two traveling women . . . this evening just became a little more entertaining. "So, what did you see in Amsterdam?" Jill asks the bunk mates.

"Well, we are from China. I come over here with my parents before meeting up with my friend, Kai Chu." She gestures towards the shy friend with red streaks accenting her long gorgeous hair. "So, my-ummm, parents took me to see some places . . . . one place they took me (She starts to grin, making jovial eye contact with both Mia and Jill in a predictable sequence. She stops and thinks), they took me to sex show." After completing her sentence she looks pleased she's able to translate her story to English for Jill and Mia. She sits, smiling, and nodding her head sweetly.

Jill looks at Mia. Mia looks at Jill. They can't suppress the smiles that surface. "Ummm, did you say, sex show?" Mia asks, curious and confused.

"Yessss, that's uuuh, right. We went to Amsterdam to the red ummm, light district, and my parents want me to learn about sex, so we saw a-uh sex show," Yang responds. Her voice rises and falls so she sounds as if she's in between singing a song and just ordinary talking.

Jill has to suck in a deep breath to control her laughter. She doesn't want Yang Sun to think she's laughing at her, but the visual in Jill's head of a young woman in line with her mother and father to watch some sort of red light sex show is hysterical. She won't dare look over at Mia, because she would surely crack, and start to laugh again.

Mia continues to keep the conversation alive. "What did you see in the sex show?" Mia's voice also starts to rise a few octaves, as she tries to control her own need to laugh.

Yang stretches her back, dangling her legs over the edge of her bed. "Ohhhh, you know. Like uh, the man and the woman, and they have sex on the stage, and the people watch. You know, a sex show." She explains casually.

At that moment, Kai Chu pulls a tightly squeezed shoe off a sore and sweaty foot. This breaks the focus on Yang and the family's bonding over a sex show, because the smell of Kai's foot is so potent it triggers Mia's gag reflex. Jill slides back on her bed to try to move slightly further from the source of the powerful stench. Then, off with the other shoe. Mia turns to Yang, and to her horror sees that now Yang is joining her friend in the removal of her sockless feet from very smelly canvas sneakers. Mia deduces that the women must have walked for miles, over days, in shoes without socks. The stench is unbearable, and Mia has to act quickly to escape the cheese scented bacterial aroma.

"So, Jill, we need to get back to the village to meet your friend, remember (wink, wink)? I almost forgot it's time for us to go. We'll leave you two, so you can unpack and have a nice shower and stuff. We'll visit more tonight then."

In two beats, Jill and Mia are hiking up the stairs, distressed to discover the cheese and feet smell has taken over the entire down stairs. Once at the top of the stairs, they both double over and take a long full smell-free breath.

A burst of laughter, and a bee-line to the outside air is in motion.

"What the hell? They look so clean and healthy! How can they make that smell?"

"I've never smelled anything like that in my life. I couldn't even breathe!"

"Sex show?"

Delight paired with horror prove to be a perfect distraction. They continue away from the hostel and back towards town. When they reach the middle part of the lone main street of Zermatt, Mia and Jill slow to gape at the details and opportunities of the quaint world class city.

Strolling by shop window after shop window; aged, and shut down for the in-between times of the seasons. Swiss Alpine décor drips from every awning, door, and window. Dark paneled wood with flowers and swirly patterns painted on shutters distract her from her immediate company. If Jill wanted to; she could pretend she's been transported back to another time and place, somewhere in some epic movie with hobbits or princes. The flags that are strewn across buildings are representative of regions Jill isn't familiar with.

"So, what do you want to do? What should we do tonight? I can't go back to that room." Mia grumbles quietly, while passing the tenth closed shop in a row.

"Maybe they took a shower, and the smell will air out," Jill retorts, trying to be positive.

"The smell is in their shoes," whines Mia.

"Okay, how about this? When they fall asleep tonight, I will steal their stank-shoes and put them outside." It's the best Jill can think to offer, she wants the accountability, since it's her wish to be in this lazy, little town.

"Eeeeww, no way. You can't touch those! They are so bad!" Mia laughs, shaking her head in disapproval.

"I'll do it for you, Mia! Yeng and Kai are cool girls, though. I like them," Jill says, pulling her friend out of her sullen mood. "You're hungry."

Mia thinks. "I like them too. Yeah, I'm starting to get pretty hungry. No McDonalds!"

"I think there's a grocery store up ahead. We can check it out." Jill answers.

Things aren't as convenient here in the Alps. Jill thinks of McDonalds, she wouldn't mind a six-piece chicken nugget and a fry. Lately, they've been eating so light, she always feels mildly hungry. Even her pants are starting to hang lower on her hips.

"What can we get at the grocery store? We don't have a kitchen. I'm kind of over bread and sandwich meat."

"It'll be fine. Besides it will be cool to check out a Swiss grocery store. We can get some beer, and sit by the river this afternoon." Jill offers, redirecting her friend's negative focus.

When they reach the grocery store, they're encouraged to see people drifting about inside. The town is so empty it's starting to feel like a backdrop for a spooky movie. All the packages of food are in a different language, and difficult to identify. Crackers are distinguishable, and so is a jar of olives. Jill wanders past a shelf of hard liquor, and ponders bringing some back to the States. Mia's left behind, stuck on the products in the cosmetic aisle. She examines a glass bottle of shampoo with some sort of herb painted on the side. Jill continues on, giving up on trying to pick out a nice bottle of whatever it is she's admiring. She finds herself walking past the frozen foods. Then she notices the frozen dinners. They have pictures of the dinners on the covers.

"Mia, we can get frozen dinners tonight. It's good and cheap!"

"Just like you, Jill." Mia shouts back, before joining Jill at the freezer case.

After several minutes, each woman selects a tasty frozen entrée. They pick up a single bottle of apple juice. Mia grabs a six pack of Heineken, and they check out.

"Wow, seven dollars for one frozen dinner. That's intense. Are you sure they have a microwave at the hostel? I'm starving." Mia comments, while they back track in the direction they've come from.

"I promise. I know I saw a microwave there. We're good, Mia, don't stress."

Hunger takes over, and the calm talkative walk there is replaced by a more focused and urgent walk back. It took thirty minutes to walk back to the Matterhorn Hostel. Once inside, the devastation sets in.

"Jill, where is this microwave? You were wrong." Mia whispers in a sad, hungry voice.

Jill rushes from room to room on the first floor, then she fumbles down the stairs. She runs to the front desk and dings the little reception bell, which is decorated in a formal edelweiss style. The older man appears, looking irritated and disinterested in Jill's issue.

"Hello, Madame, how can I help you?" His tone is brass.

"I was wondering if you have a microwave we can use?" Jill holds up her frozen dinner, pointing to it, in hopes the prop might inspire the inn keeper. He frowns and shakes his head no.

"I am sorry, we don't use microwaves here." He sees the hopeless look stiffen Jill's face. Next, he notices the scorned, and infuriated look of Mia glaring at her companion. He turns to avoid a situation where he may have to help them further. Jill tragically watches the man turn and disappear into his back office. She starts to sweat, feeling put on the spot. She can't accept that this is the final outcome, that she's failed her mission. That she and Mia will starve and have lost a total of fourteen dollars due to her hasty judgment. She can't believe her friend tried to warn her, and that she argued, and pushed the frozen entrees, and the long hungry walk back to the hostel with the stinky feet smell. Jill has to stomach the hard fact that this is a big problem, and it's all her fault. She turns to her companion, ready to eat the frozen blame that's served with a side of stupidity.

"Oh, my, God Jill. Really? You said you saw a microwave for sure? We're on a budget. That just cost me seven dollars."

Desperate and hungry, and wanting to make things right for her friend, Jill decides to "cowgirl up". "I can fix this, Mia. Give me the food."

"What are you going to do?" Mia asks with less anger and more curiosity.

"I'm going to return it, get our money back, and get us some dinner." Jill answers, hoping to reconcile all present issues.

Mia looks doubtful, and confused. "You can't return food to a grocery store."

"I can, and I will. They have to take it back, we can't use it."

"But, seriously, it's a frozen dinner, and it's half melted from the thirty minute walk through town. If you take it back, it will be completely thawed. You're really going to try to return it?" Mia's anger is replaced by humor, thinking of Jill trying to return thawed frozen dinners to a Swiss grocery cashier. Part of her wants to witness the event, but the other part wants to avoid the embarrassing situation at all cost. "Seriously, Jill, you can't do that."

"I'll do it." Jill states with firmness, terrified that she's pledged to do the most irrational and uncomfortable thing she's ever thought to do in her life. "Yes, here, give me the dinner. I'll be back in an hour."

She knows to make it right, she can't ask her friend to do the round trip hour-long walk again. She knows she will have to make the long shameful journey alone, with nothing but a plastic grocery bag of almost thawed dinner entrees. Even though it's only a frozen dinner; Jill is so hungry, and the meal sounds so perfect. She salivated over the prospect of it the entire walk back to the hostel. She mourns the loss of her Salisbury steak and potato meal, and with one foot after the other, makes the pilgrimage back to the store. Mia lets Jill go, knowing Jill deserves to endure the aftermath of her flawed judgment. Plus it makes her feel a little better about being hungry.

Just like Mia predicted, the dinners are about ninety percent thawed, and dripping with condensation. They've been jostled about in the bag for an hour now. Jill finally passes through the automatic grocery doors. She sprints for the cashier in hopes of salvaging the final ten percent of frozen material. The cashier's disturbed and concerned by the wild-eyed American woman clutching a plastic bag with damp items. Dinners hanging in the balance of space, dangling from her enclosed fist while a camera knocks into it continuously. The cashier forces a casual smile, to help encourage

Jill to relax and communicate. Jill starts to tremble slightly from embarrassment at the unusual request. She decides honesty will work the best.

She steps forward, as if she's preparing to make a formalized speech. "Hi, my name is Jill and I am here from America." The awkwardness ascends to a new level. "I thought my hostel had a microwave to cook these dinners, but it doesn't." The cashier follows Jill's story intently. "I can't eat these dinners. I was wondering if I could return them, or trade them for different food."

The cashier pauses, just staring at the sweaty bag. Jill is afraid to set the entrees down on the counter, as if this act requires permission first. So for two long minutes, Jill stands, staring at the cashier, and the cashier stares at Jill and her bag, trying to decide what to do.

"Yes, of course. You can trade this food." The short cashier extends her hand to accept the inconvenient burden. She doesn't scold Jill, or laugh. She gives a kind smile, and with two clicks of the register, the drawer pops open, and fourteen dollars are placed back into Jill's timid hand.

"Oh, thank you. Thank you!" Jill starts to bow her head in a strange submissive way while she backs herself up. It's time to shop in the grand Swiss mercantile. She knows she must seem odd, but this is already odd, and it can't get any weirder. The kind and compassionate gesture of returning the cash has somehow touched Jill in a way she wasn't prepared for. She can't help but emotionally react, and it's all she can do, not to cry. Perhaps it's the hunger combined with so many miles of walking, but having unloaded the frozen dinner entrees lightens her heart, and she can now move forward to dinner, and beers by a high alpine river.

Two yogurts, a box of crackers, a basket of berries, and a half brick of cheese are nestled into her shopping basket. Jill walks back over to the imperial looking liquors on the shelf. She picks a bottle with a yellow label, and pictures of hiking men in little shorts with suspenders, they stand happily, blowing big horns. Soon she's in route to the Matterhorn hostel with dinner for her friend. She somehow feels better. She could have thrown away the meals, and lied to Mia about returning them, but she really wanted to get the money back, and redeem her good name. She really did it. She actually returned thawed out frozen dinners to a Zermatt grocery store. She impresses herself for her ethical convictions, and congratulates herself for following through. She's triumphant. After all, she is an American.

.　　　.　　　.　　　.　　　.

The clouds start to build and block patches of the ice blue sky. Jill reaches up and wipes away the sweat that's been resting on her brow since the exchange of groceries. She's nearly to the front door of the hostel when she hears a flat voice call her name.

"Jill, you have dinner!" It's Mia, and she's making the most of her time, lying out on a smooth boulder. She's facing the swollen river. She looks natural, blending well with the surroundings. She has on earth-toned layers, her silk blue scarf draped twice around her neck, and her canvas shoes wagging back and forth, pointing to the sky. The strap of her purse is pulled tight across her body, and accents her already prominent style.

"I appreciate dinner! Thanks, Jill. I should have gone with you to help. Those groceries get heavy after carrying them so far." She points to the two bags twisting around Jill's right arm. Jill continues towards Mia, until she pushes herself onto the rock to join her friend. They empty the contents of the bag onto the rock between them.

"So, it still stinks in there." Mia says, in a depressed, amused sort of way.

"I'm sorry I was so insistent that we come to Zermatt. I know it's kind of boring. I don't know, I still am really, seriously, happy that we're here. Even if it is a little boring."

Mia dips a strawberry into her tart foreign yogurt, she takes a small bite from the end. "I like it here. It's actually really amazing. I've never seen any place like this. I'm glad we're here."

Hearing Mia's approval of Zermatt turns out to be the affirmation Jill needs. She swallows a mouth full of unidentifiable white cheese. "I'm relieved you like it here. I think tomorrow we should really get out and explore. Would you be into hiking, or taking pictures?" Jill lifts her heavy thirty five millimeter camera up off her neck to reference the significance of photographing their strange journey.

"Sure, let's hike out of the town tomorrow. Let's go to the mountain." Mia answers. "There's the ski resort. You know, I was thinking about how dead the town is today. I wonder if they have a siesta."

"Siesta?"

"Yeah, you know, like when everyone takes a few hours in the middle of the day to sleep and stuff."

Jill's quiet. She isn't familiar with siestas or empty alpine villages. She dismisses the puzzle from her mind.

"We'll get some more scones and espresso, then pick up a picnic lunch for the hike." Jill shifts her weight back, propped up by her left arm. "Mia, do you mind getting the stuff from the store tomorrow?"

They giggle.

Jill's recalls the canvas stink bombs back in their room and giggles even more. "Have you seen them come out?"

Mia knows exactly who she's asking about. She kicks a small pinecone off the rock and shakes her head. The women stay in the peaceful place, watching the sun roll back behind the jagged peaks, sitting and listening to a river move itself over the virtue of alpine terrain.

When retreating back to the room; each woman holds their breath as long as they can. At some point they adapt to the potent scent of cheese and feet. Jill loses her courage; she spent it all returning frozen food this afternoon. She opts to leave the Chinese travelers shoes untouched. They fall asleep dreaming of rivers and trails and unknown places that reach for them.

·   ·   ·   ·   ·

In the morning, Mia and Jill move quietly past their new friends, looking forward to pouring their focus into a trail that ascends to mysteries hiding behind bends. A conversation needs to take place today. Neither woman feels focused enough to address the urgent issue. The problem is: they haven't discussed where exactly they are going after today. Paris is a safe choice, from there they could go anywhere. Relying on the newly familiar, this could be the next destination at hand. However, there's the constant obvious, that neither friend speaks of. Mia wants to go back to Amsterdam and indulge her interest in her red-headed fantasy. Jill isn't satisfied with her journey completely, and wants more. Her travelling days are now numbered. In less than a week, she's scheduled to go home. Mia will go to Spain to stay with relatives. Jill is hoping to fit in a quick visit to Lourdes, but she can see it would be demanding to push her friend into another unplanned side trip. Jill decides that she loves France, and if Lourdes isn't in the cards, she could easily and comfortably enjoy Paris for a few more days. She even considers going back to Amsterdam to relax with Mia, as a way of saying thanks for being supportive of her dream to see the Matterhorn. On one hand, Jill truly doesn't want to waste her final days on her "trip of a lifetime:" drinking and smoking with a bunch of men living in tents. Resting in the other hand is the notion that persuades her to be a good friend, and to participate in some socialization during her trip. She just regrets the fact that those men most definitely heard her farting in her sleep. If she could eliminate this fact from the equation, it would make it a lot easier for her to look forward to seeing them again. If only they weren't hot and adorable. Why couldn't they have been ugly and jerks? Slightly agitated, she decides to focus on her hike, the lonesome trail that climbs high into the Swiss mountain side, each step bringing her closer to the pristine and haunting vision of the great twisted peak. She squeezes her eyes tight just before kicking a pinecone somewhere along the trail amidst flowers and meadowlarks.

In the evening, Mia and Jill stay up chatting with their Chinese counterparts. They compare cultural traditions, and miles traveled. They talk more about Amsterdam sex shows, and Mia even confides in Yeng Sun and Kai Chu about her crush on Paul. Kai Chu is scheduled to be married this fall. She's visiting two more continents before she returns back to China and her groom. Yeng is starting her career in education when she returns home. Night is closing in, and all four bunk mates wiggle down into their sleeping bags, now silent in the darkness of the cave-like room.

The next day, it's the desire for Swiss espresso which finally persuades Mia and Jill to shed the warm cocoons that grant them the solitude they're often deprived of. It's cool in the early morning hours. Mia looks over at Yeng Sun and Kai Chu. Yeng is spooning a giant "Hello Kitty" pillow, while Kai Chu has a decent sized puddle of drool collecting below her mouth. Mia and Jill desperately want to sneak out, before their roommates wake up. It isn't that they didn't want to visit more, or that they don't like the women. It's more of an opportunity to avoid having to say goodbye. Saying goodbye is a common dislike that Mia and Jill share. This shared thought process guides them quickly and stealthily out of the intimate room on tiptoes. Backpacks tightly welded to shoulders with straps, and two bulky camera's flailing from Jill's neck, signify that the time to depart is upon them. With one last walk through the lazy little alpine town, two small women with great big backpacks work their way back to the train station, only stopping for coffee and strudel to go.

Huit

Once boarded on the train, the long day of traveling unfurls before them. If they transition smoothly between trains, they might arrive to Paris close to five in the evening. This time, there are no hostels or hotels booked for them. They've left this leg of their journey to chance, assuming they will go where they want. Throughout the day, Mia's anxiety starts to build until it develops into a full blown panic. She can't relax not knowing what will happen when they reach Paris.

"We'll be fine. Let's just spend the night in the train station, again. We'll save so much money." Jill suggests.

For reasons, they don't quite understand, by Mia and Jill, they have a compulsion to spend as little money as possible. It seems odd to want to be without shelter all night in a foreign country, but Mia and Jill are on a roll. Their frugality has carved itself, snowballing away from them, collecting bad judgments as it goes. When they add the night's lodging saved by sleeping in random men's tents and the squatting in a train depot, they realize they can easily get around without spending too much money. Jill's suggestion somehow relieves Mia, and she settles into her train car seat, imagining another adventuresome night, surviving the streets of Paris, at their post in the brightly-lit train station with friendly custodians named

Cedric who would buy them breakfast in the morning. The past evenings had provided both women with plenty of sleep, and the long day on the train gave them more than enough rest. They can effortlessly stay awake all night and have a new adventure. The uneventful days in Zermatt leave both women craving excitement and risk.

Mia looks at Jill and nods, "Really? You would do it? All night in the train station again?"

Jill grins with mischief, "Of course I would. I had so much fun. Why not?"

"I don't know, it's kind of crazy, and kind of stupid."

Jill considers this concept. It probably is entirely stupid for a twenty year old women to lurk around an empty train station all night long. Anything can happen. She thinks about nine-one-one. In the States, that was who to call for help. A vulnerable sensation pushes up against her confidence, when she realizes she has no idea how to find help in Paris if she were in trouble. She shivers at the thought, then reasons the fun is worth the risk. They are adventurers now.

"Well, let's agree to it, then. We'll try to spend the night at the train station. If it doesn't work out, there are so many hostels and hotels in Paris. We can have a plan A, B, and C."

"I'm in." Mia says, her eyes curve at the corners with mischief. Her tone drops. It's time, they can't avoid the conversation any longer. "So, tonight I'll hang out with you in Paris, but tomorrow I really want to go back to Amsterdam. I got a text from Paul and he cut his hair! His gorgeous red hair. I have to go see."

Jill is quiet, she doesn't answer right away.

"So, is it okay with you if we go back to Amsterdam?" Mia's unsure of how else to ask.

The word "we" suddenly strikes Jill with a new thought. Deep down, she just doesn't want to give up her last days in Europe to a group of guys partying in a campground, whom she'll never see again. She starts to wind the strap of her camera around her fingers as she thinks. Then, she feels sure. "I think you should go to Amsterdam, and I should stay in Paris."

Mia gives Jill a troubled look. "I can't leave you in Paris." Mia looks defeated, she feels how much she just really wants to go see Paul and the other Irishmen. She even misses annoying Addison.

"No, really. You should go meet the guys. I'll stay here by myself for just one extra night. There are so many things I still want to see in Paris."

"Like what?" Mia's eyes blink, considering the idea of a temporary separation.

"I really want to go back to the Louvre, and there are a couple cathedrals I really want to check out. I just want to go around the city and work on my photography."

Mia understands and gives her friend a genuine smile. The prospect of traveling alone is enticing, and would be good for both of them. They're in need of some time alone. There's been so much compromising and accommodating. Jill will be able to put on her double cameras and travel pouch without getting that judgmental look from Mia. Mia can go where she wants without keeping tabs on the status of her perpetually challenged friend. This would be their time.

The hum of the train engine groans to a stop at the Gar De Lyon station. Within minutes both women are standing on the platform, cameras and backpacks secured to their person. Mia and Jill scan the station with a twinkle of deviant intention. "I'm not sure this station will work for tonight." whispers Mia.

"Let's go to the Nord. It's only five right now. What's the plan?"

"Pizza?"

"Perfect."

Mia smiles, she always loves when they converse in one word sentences. Jill and Mia navigate through the bustle of the crowded station, and over to a far corner where a small café sells pizza by the slice, pasta by the pound, and salad. Mia explores the menu, referencing the prices instead of the food content. Six euro, eight euro, fourteen euro, and there it is: four euro.

She steps up to the counter. "Ummm, s'il vous plait fromage pizza?" Her voice waivers, doubting her ability to order the slice. She decides to offer the cashier a visual aid, and uses her finger to point to the slices of cheese pizza under the heated lights in the glass display case.

The young man working the register answers happily, "Oui mademoiselle, une tranche de pizza au fromage. Quelque chose à boire miss."

Mia isn't sure what he said, but he seems confident enough, so she replies, "s'il vous plait . . . au revoir." She can tell by his expression, she didn't answer right. All she can do is wait for him to try again.

"Un verre?"

She just stares, holding out her money with a determined look.

"Un verre." This time he repeats with pronunciation and it sounds more like a statement, instead of a question. Then he mimics a person drinking a glass of water. Faking the drinking, tipping back his imaginary glass.

Mia's face turns red. She looks at the mineral waters and juices behind him on the shelf. Her eyes roll back as she struggles to think of the right way to ask for the bottled water. She feels his patience wear thin, she points and simply says, "water." She doesn't even try to add the "s'il vous plait," at the end of her request. She feels unworthy.

She passes the young man her cash, and he places the change gently in her hand. She avoids his eyes. He serves her the slice of cheese pizza and a room temperature bottle of water. Jill steps up directly behind Mia. Jill's less intimidated by the young Frenchman.

"I'll have the same." She points to Mia and nods her head, to help him interpret her obvious request. She holds out the five euros, and takes her meal, before heading off to catch up to Mia who's now at the opposite end of the pizza counter, trying to find a quiet and discrete corner to enjoy her modest dinner. Jill slides in next to her on a bench that's half tucked under the cafeteria-style table.

"That guy was a jerk, he really pissed me off." Mia grumbles, before taking a big cheesy bite.

"That guy? He was nice, I didn't see him say anything rude or anything." Jill answers while sprinkling generous amounts of parmesan onto her pizza. Jill contently sets down the parmesan and lifts up her bottle of tepid water. She can't help but smile at the dopey way Mia's embarrassed herself.

"Don't stress so much. You did great ordering in French. I'm proud of you. Remember when we were back at the Children's Museum and I had that kid's book about learning French. I can't believe you learned all those words. Now here we are, using them in France!" Jill takes a big bite of pizza, reveling in the last part of her sentence. Mia smiles too. Jill knows just what to say. They linger on the bench for close to an hour, just watching the commuter crowd leaving the city to return home. The traffic reminds Jill of San Francisco, and for a few minutes she becomes intensely homesick. Mia sees the distant melancholy stare and it jolts her out of her own daydream that includes Paul and a tent, and all the possibilities of young love. Mia stands up, catching Jill's attention.

"We should go."

"It's only six thirty. We'll be stuck at the train station for hours if we go there now."

"I know. Let's go walk, find a bar somewhere. Oooh, shopping, ice cream?" Mia has all the trigger words figured out for her Jill, and they work like magic.

"Okay." Jill stands up, and hoists her backpack up high onto her shoulders. Like a soldier, she boldly reaches back, grabbing her hip straps and buckling them in one sweeping motion. Mia follows Jill through the busy station and out into the faint Spring night. The fresh air crashes against them and smells of the city prick their senses. Mia looks to her right, then to her left, she stops and turns to check on Jill. Then she proceeds forward, across the street, and over in a direction that offers more lights and, hopefully, stores and ice cream parlors. Jill walks behind Mia instead of beside her. This formation feels more comfortable and allows the women to walk silently, losing themselves in thought, and focusing on where they will go. The fun of a night trying to be homeless has somehow evaded them. A tired anxiousness is starting to settle at the pit of Mia's stomach. Despite the fact that Paris is gorgeous, a subtle undertone of danger rivets her thinking, and casts a shadow over her sense of the city.

The first time she became aware of the unsettling feeling was during the first fifteen minutes upon arriving in Paris, when the hippie warned them about walking around after dark. She decides if she sees a reasonable looking hotel she'll go in and see about a room. They walk past a fancy restaurant filled with couples and students enjoying a level of cuisine that is unfamiliar to the California twenty year olds. Soon they've walked close to a mile without finding a decent place to hang out and explore. Mia sits down on a bench which marks a metro entrance. Jill joins her.

"I know," Jill offers, with a renewed burst of inspiration.

Mia looks at her, hoping the plan will be good.

"Let's cruise around on the Metro, just see where it goes."

Mia tries to imagine this activity. After a day on the train, the metro hardly seems thrilling. But, then, she shrugs her shoulders and concludes, "Why not?"

Soon the two friends are climbing aboard a peculiar train system that looks like it extends beyond the very end of the metro map. This route is unknown, and they're intrigued by what might lie beyond the edge of the city. The metro is bright, and the train has only a few other passengers. For a few dollars, they can sit in a warm, well-lit, safe environment. Mia's starting to catch on to the brilliance of the plan. She's even starting to feel a little excited about the possibility of the night and its options.

The train pushes its way through tunnels, then merges with a railway that lifts above the ground. They find themselves approaching a residential area. It's almost eight, and the neighborhoods look empty and hollow.

"We did it, we made it to the end of the metro map," Jill shouts gleefully.

They're now the only passengers, and the train is progressively slowing down. All of the sudden it squeals to a loud stop.

"I think we're at the end of the track. Should we get out?"

Mia starts to fidget with her backpack straps, "I don't know?" She starts to look around, getting her bearings for where they might be. "We're in the middle of nowhere." She whispers even though there's no one to hear them. "Let's just stay and wait until we can go back into Paris."

Jill nods in agreement. The two women sit, and sit even more. They tap their feet, and fuss over their hair a little. The train shows no sign of departing any time soon. They wait, continuing to sit, awaiting the trip back.

"So, I think this train might just be parked here for the night." Mia reveals what they both are thinking.

Caught by surprise, a metro employee taps on the door of the train car before he slides it open. He doesn't enter, but holds the attention of both Mia and Jill. " Bonjour, sont les amoureux de sortir?"

Jill's tired, and isn't even going to try to speak in French. "We took the wrong train, we are waiting to go back to the metro station."

The man who works for the metro presses the folds and buttons on the collar of his shirt before replying mechanically. "This train stays here at night. You have to get off and catch the ten-thirty train to go back. It is the last train, so you want to make sure not to miss it." He speaks slowly, stretching each vowel. He leans in and holds the door, waiting for the women to climb off his train.

"Yeah, okay, let's get off, I guess." Mia stands up and drags her pack behind her, before lifting it to exit the train.

Jill trails close behind, not wanting to be separated for a second. If they became separated now, they have no means to find one another. After stepping off; the man reaches his hand into the car, shuts the lights off, and latches the door behind them. He continues down the row of cars, repeating his night's work. Mia and Jill walk in the opposite direction. They see a train shelter with a roof and glass walls. They enter the small building and rest their packs on the wooden slats of a wooden bench. The man has vanished. Mia and Jill aren't concerned with him, and would prefer not to cross paths with him again. Instead they explore their little shelter. Another map of the metro system is fastened to the wall, it has a bold yellow dot marking their location. They can hear crickets chirping and a soft wind blowing through tall grass just beyond their field of vision, hidden by the uncertain night. Things feel peaceful, and they're alone together to relax and think.

"I wish we had a beer." Jill says, thinking about how to improve the situation. She looks at her watch, "We have close to two hours."

"We can go for a walk around the neighborhood, they might have a corner store or a place to get beer." Jill speaks with hesitation, unsure if a walk is a good choice. The neighborhood seems nice enough, but the quiet desolation makes her feel uneasy. She sits back on the bench, extending her legs and pointing her toes, she reclines herself against the cool glass wall. They look out at the dark field, not speaking, just waiting. They aren't sure what they're waiting for, but the potential for something to happen is there, so they want to be ready. The lights are turned off and the station is dark. There's only one light left, which illuminates the small box of a shelter they're now within. This sets an eerie portrait, everything in the background is dim and colorless.

Something catches Mia's attention. There lurking just out of range of her primary vision is a figure. She keeps still, not wanting to scare Jill. She continues to stare ahead, trying to seem unaware of the mysterious company. She's stiff, her breathing is calm, and from what she can determine, the figure isn't trying to creep. It's simply walking slowly towards them. Jill jumps, she realizes there's a man approaching.

Mia slides her body close to her friend. "Act cool, we're okay." She whispers to Jill.

One singular man in a tan trench coat, wearing a black tie enters the small train shelter. Thoughts race through Mia's mind. She wonders why he's there. It's still an hour until the next train is expected. She wonders what his intentions are and why he's walking alone late at night.

"Bonjour." He smiles hungrily at the poised women. He has a tan complexion and a thick accent.

Mia speaks up. She's good at confrontations, and it's natural for her to drive the boat through treacherous waters. "Hi," she answers with a bold coolness. Despite her small feminine frame, she's strong, and has the ability to reveal that strength when needed, especially around pushy men.

He steps in closer, examining the women. They can see he's still deciding what to say. "Are you waiting for the train?"

Mia nods. "Yes, and our friends are meeting us here in fifteen minutes."

He looks long and slow at Jill, then turns and gives an equally creepy look to Mia. "Oh, okay. Do you know when the train is coming?"

"Yeah, the train will be here in about forty five minutes." She doesn't smile or act cordial when replying. Silence fills the space, but the energy intensifies between the three figures. He lingers for close to ten minutes, watching, and thinking over something in his head. He turns to the women and tells them, "Goodnight."

He leaves the shelter but stays off to the side, close to thirty feet away from the boarding divider. The man remains in this spot for close to five minutes. He appears to be staring out at the empty field, occasionally checking his watch. Soon he's gone, disappearing into the unknown abyss of night. Jill and Mia don't speak for another fifteen minutes. They both want to listen and watch, until they feel certain he's gone.

"Screw this, Jill, I have a bad feeling about this place. We need to get out of here."

The panic and urgency strikes a chord within Jill, and she starts to shiver from the chill and stress of the evening.

"Jill, look!"

Another form hidden in the darkness is now making it's way to the shelter. Mia feels like a fish in a fish bowl, with the light shining in through the glass. In desperate fright, Jill grabs hold of Mia's arm tightly, and all they can do is wait, frozen, until whoever's out there moves into the light. After all the agony, a moment of bliss. Mia jabs Jill in the side. "Look, he's a kid!"

Jill looks across the dividing platform and sees the youthful silhouette making his way to the shelter. Jill stands up, and by the time she smooths the crease in her pants, he's joining them in the confinement of the fish bowl.

"Hi." Jill gives him a huge goofy grin. The boy looks like he might be sixteen or seventeen. He has a blue jacket and a blue backpack slung over one shoulder. He gives her a reserved smile, and his brown eyes reflect the fluorescent lights buzzing at the top of the enclosure. The boy is less thrilled to find the women. He's a little taken aback by how abnormally happy they are to see him. He lifts his hand to wave hello, but decides to remain quiet for the time being. Jill isn't deterred by his anti-social demeanor. She understands that it's an unrealistic judgment to believe they would be safe now that a teenage boy has joined them, but somehow, in her desperate reasoning, she's confident they are now safe thanks to this boy. She also decides it's okay if she seems silly or odd, and feels free to act and speak however she wants. So, she tries to initiate a conversation with her angel-boy who brings her so much comfort.

"We are Americans," Jill gives him a big, exaggerated thumbs up.

Mia can't help but laugh at the terrible way Jill is behaving. She looks like such a huge American jackass right this second.

The boy stares at her. He keeps his arms stiff, hands down at his sides. Mia recognizes the expression on his face. He was looking at them, the way they were looking at the man with the trench coat.

"We got lost, and have been stuck here for almost two hours. Do you live here? Are you going to Paris? Are we still in Paris?"

The boy's eyes grow wide as he tries to assess the madness that he's stumbled upon. "I can speak some English, and will try to answer you." The young teen offers in defense.

He stands in the bus stop, shifting his weight from foot to foot to stay warm. He looks down the train tracks, watching for the train, instead of at Mia or Jill. He speaks gently and slowly, while keeping his gaze up the tracks. "So, you got lost. I'm sorry. This train will take you back to the city."

Jill decides to confess their hidden agendas to the blessing that is the brown-eyed boy. Unsure if she likes the French boy because he isn't the scary man, or because he's another human to lighten the tension between Mia and Jill. For now, it doesn't matter. He's here, and Jill likes it.

"We don't have a place to stay tonight!" She announces gleefully, hoping to strike up a conversation which might offer them some sort of assistance.

The boy's eyebrow arches up in a curious thought, he can't figure out what these women want from him. He tries to answer politely. "There are hotels near the city center, I think you can find one still. It's only ten."

This is when Jill realizes the boy is not a Cedric. She isn't sure if he will even visit with them. She looks over at Mia, who looks regretful that Jill is informing the young teen that they were lost without any place to stay. She can't believe Jill is divulging such information to a random person they've met only minutes before. Mia decides to just avoid eye contact with the polite young man who only wishes to keep to himself.

Jill continues. "Do you know of any hostels? Where are you going right now?" Jill deduces, since he's leaving a neighborhood, he must be going out somewhere.

"I am going home. My mother is expecting me."

"Oh." Jill responds thoughtfully. She decides it's enough that he is just there. His existence makes the whole area seem a lot less creepy.

The distant rumble of a train sounds before they can see it. Then the tracks start to vibrate, and finally the train pulls into the station. Jill, Mia, and the young man spring forward, prepped and ready to move on from the stagnant windowed shelter. They all scramble into one train car. The warmth and light in the car is like a big hug for Mia. She only wants to leave this place. She lets her head rest against the back of the seat, laying her backpack on the floor so she can prop her feet on it and recline. She pulls her scarf up around her neck and lowers her chin down into it, trying to use her body language to communicate to Jill and the boy that she doesn't want to talk. All she wants is to put the situation behind her. She focuses on the corner of the train car where the wall and ceiling meet. She thinks of Paris, and resigns herself to yet another train ride.

Jill sits across from the boy, and awkwardly smiles at him. He gives them a few long looks, and Jill can see he's deep in thought. She assumes he might be trying to figure out a way to help them. Jill discovers she really wants someone to help them . . . anyone to help them, because she's starting to grow tired of always having to help herself. All the navigating, currency exchange, reservations, and keeping the relationship with her travel companion civil, is exhausting. It's getting late, they have no plan for the evening, and she just doesn't want to deal with any of it. She wants to have fun and relax, to enjoy her vacation. She suspects she's missing the point, why she came, and what she wants out of her trip. She turns and faces Mia, quietly watching, and wishing she had more to offer her friend. If she was better at speaking the language, or interpreting the art, or understanding the maps, she could be more useful. She lets out a depressed sigh that helps her feel a little better.

The train takes them all the way to the main depot. The boy exits the car. He turns to say goodnight. Jill waves goodbye and is a little sad to see him go. Mia and Jill step off the train and walk lightheartedly down the dividing platform. Other trains pull into the immense station. Two trains are parked, and shut down. The other is boarding passengers. The station is big, and inviting. The warmth and gold lighting give them a sense of security. Jill trails behind Mia as they walk leisurely through the slow pace of the late evening.

"How many train stations have we been to today?" Mia asks, her voice reflecting the rise in her mood.

"Well, if you don't count the metro station points, this would be our fourth train station. We're on a train station tour!" Jill answers, encouraged by the thought.

"I'm pretty much over that tour, Jill," Mia laughs. "Do you really want to stay the night here?" Her tone dips slightly and she scans the perimeter of the building. Like magic, the second after she finishes her sentence, a groan bounces from the walls with the dimming of the station lights. All of the sudden all the people who are roaming the train depot stop, and start heading for the big official doors which lead to the exit. The sound of the power shutting down, and the dimming of the station lights catch Mia by surprise.

She grabs Jill by the arm. "Jill, what's happening?"

On some level she knows what's happening, she just refuses to accept it. The station is obviously closing, and everyone inside has to leave. They have to leave. But, leave for where? Her thoughts rush in and anxiety overwhelms her ability to reason.

Her breathing shortens. "Jill, what are we going to do now?"

Mia doesn't expect Jill to have the answers, but she's angry, and wants someone to deal with this screwed-up situation. After being stranded in some shady train stop in the middle of nowhere with Jill, she's now, in no mood for another sequence of events that have wrapped her up in this unfortunate evening.

"Ummm, I don't know. Let's just wait and see. We're not sure they're closing," Jill responds, hoping for the best.

An older man with a broom and a bag of trash stops and shares something in French, before pointing at the doors. They get the meaning, even though they can't decipher the message. As if his finger is some sort of imaginary force, the girls feel themselves being pushed by his intensity.

With defeat spreading over their ideas, they give up on the fantasy of playing in a train depot all night long. They're in a small group of seven, who are the last of the public to leave the station. Once outside, the night traffic growls and threatens with ill intention. Standing on the sidewalk, Jill and Mia are greeted by a fleet of taxi's lining up. Jill wants a taxi, so does Mia, but they can't figure out where to tell the taxi to take them. They don't even really know where they are, just somewhere, kicked out, onto the streets of Paris at eleven at night. Jill turns to Mia. Mia turns to Jill. They stare, thinking fast to come up with a master plan.

"This time you're not arguing with me, Jill. We're finding a hotel. We tried to have an adventure tonight. It didn't work. That's okay. Let's just focus on finding a place to sleep. Come on, let's start walking."

Jill's glad Mia's taking control. She's tired, and doesn't feel like putting together some sort of sideways, complicated plan. Without saying a word, both women take to a fast and directionless walk down an empty Parisian sidewalk. Jill remains quiet and Mia thinks. Five minutes pass and they can no longer see the train depot that had a funny way of filling the nightscape.

Mia stops, so does Jill. "I'm getting out my phone." She states with the firmness of a marine sergeant.

Mia has a special cell phone her mom had purchased for her trip. The phone has the ability to call overseas. Even though her phone is capable of it, her mother had warned her only to use it for emergencies and for calls to check in every couple of days. From what they understood, it cost around thirty to forty dollars to make a call. There, huddled in the middle of an empty street, they call Mia's mom. They wait silently. Mia's mom answers on the line.

"Mom." Mia's voice waivers with emotion, afraid, embarrassed, and angry that she has to tell her mom they screwed up. "Mom, we're in Paris. Yes, it's late, close to midnight. On the street. We need to find a place to stay tonight. Can you go online, and find a hostel close by?"

Jill listens as Mia pauses to get information and instruction from her mother.

"Yes, we are, umm, I don't know, by the train station."

Jill looks around, hoping to see a street sign, or a clue to the whereabouts of their location. Everything looks dark, empty, and strange.

"Okay, okay, yes, Mom. I love you, too. Okay. Bye." Mia clicks the phone shut, and slips it into her pocket. She turns to Jill, still looking emotional from having heard her mother's voice.

Jill's glad she isn't the only one who can feel homesick. Mia squares her shoulders, and sucks in a long clean breath before sharing her information. "My mom is going to go online. She's going to try to find us a place for tonight."

Jill nods, grateful for Mia's mother. In the mean time they start to walk again. They have nothing else to do. The phone rings from Mia's pocket.

"Hello, yes, okay. Uh, huh. Mom, thank you so much. I will. Okay, I'll call you when we get there. Rue Guynemer, The Round World Hostel." Again, the phone is shoved back onto Mia's pocket. She turns to Jill. "We have a room booked for both of us. My mom paid for it already. It's at The Round World Hostel on Rue Guynemer."

Jill throws her arms around Mia. "Thanks, Mia. I'm sorry."

Mia's troubled expression falls from her face as the TLC from her mother fills her heavy heart with comfort and security. Even in the middle of the night on a cold street corner in a foreign land, a mother's love conquers the grim situation. She winks, and returns the hug.

"My mom said the street is directly off of the train depot. We just have to back track a little. We'll just walk a couple of blocks to the hostel."

"Oh, thank you, Jesus!" Jill cries out dramatically, feeling enticed to make noise, since the streets are empty. With a kick in their step; they back track all the way to the train station. They easily find the route that will take them to the hostel and continue on their merry way. Fifteen minutes pass, then twenty five. Soon forty minutes have gone by, and they continue to walk tirelessly down Rue Guynemer. .

"This isn't right." Mia whispers.

Twenty more minutes pass, they grow more serious, wondering why they haven't found the hostel yet. The road keeps going forever, with no end in sight. "We must have passed it, and I didn't notice. I think we've gone too far."

"No way, not possible. We've been reading every sign and looking at every building on the street."

"I think we should go back." Mia repeats.

"But, what if you're wrong? Then we have to turn around again. We've been traveling in circles all night," Jill mutters.

"So what do you want to do?" challenges Mia.

"There." Jill points to a small corner pub, with two faint lights glowing from within. "There are people in there, we can ask them for directions."

"That place looks sketchy," Mia protests.

"Walking up and down this crazy French street in the middle of the night is sketchy. I won't do it, unless we make sure there's a hostel somewhere on this road, and we need to get better directions."

Mia decides Jill's request is sensible enough. So down to the end of the block they walk, their backpacks growing heavier with each grueling step. Mia goes first, throwing open the old obscure door with the stained glass triangle. Jill pushes through, right behind her, looking forward to a chair and shelter from the chilled evening air. Despite coming in from the darkness of night, they both have to squint their eyes to adjust to the low lighted ambience of the sunken haunt.

First they see the bartender. They shuffle past bistro tables until they reach the small L shaped bar. The bartender's stacking shot glasses on a shelf opposite the women. He doesn't greet them immediately. Jill and Mia stand and wait politely. Three other men are in the quiet bar at this hour. One man is sitting at the bar on the other length of the L. The other two men are sitting at table in the corner, which is pushed up against dark wooden walls. Jill looks up, then reviews the outline of the drinking establishment. She can't quite decide what's strange about the room, until she takes a light inventory. The bar doesn't have light fixtures, instead it has two floor lamps on either side of the seating area. There's also a faint light coming up from behind the bar. Music is playing on an aged sound system that produces a gravelly feedback which bleeds into the songs. A minute breezes by, the bartender continues to ignore them. One of the men at the tables stands up and greets the downtrodden women.

"Bonjour." He waves his hand, then flips his dark hair back from his face. Jill's more encouraged by the warm gesture, while Mia is in no mood to small talk with the stranger in the rude bar. Mia rolls her eyes and refocuses them to the backside of the unfriendly bartender. Jill waves at the man.

"Are you Americans?" He points at their backpacks.

"Yes, we're actually here because we need to find our hostel, and we can't find it on this crazy street."

"Oh?" The dark haired man with the crafty eyes looks more interested.

Mia submits to the attention, realizing he may be their last hope for help. She's desperate, and suspects they must be getting closer to wherever it was they're trying to get to.

"Come and sit with me, and I'll try to give you the directions. Poor things. You look tired. Can I buy you a drink?"

With this suggestion, he receives smiles from both Jill and Mia. If Mia has a soft spot, it's for presents. She loves when people give her things. It reminds her that she is worth giving things to, and that makes her happy. Jill's happy because Mia's happy, and they are almost done being lost for the night. The evening's been so complicated, she even forgot to think about tomorrow. Mia would be leaving her alone here. Would that be okay? She couldn't think of it now. They have the task of finding shelter to deal with.

"Hello, I am Antonin." The friendly stranger, holds out his hand which looks eager and suspicious.

"Hi." Mia shakes.

Antonin leans in to kiss her cheek.

"Hey." Jill shakes.

Antonin leans in to kiss her cheek.

"And your names are?"

Jill blushes for forgetting common formalities. The French have a way of making her feel self-conscious and nervous. The sad truth is that both women are reluctant to share their names with him. Something about him isn't right. He's too inquisitive.

"I can help you get to your hostel. Where are you going? Hold on. Trois bières trou du cul," he calls to the bartender. "Sorry. Yes, tell me what you need. I can help you."

Mia looks at Jill. Jill's waiting for the okay look, before she shares any more facts about themselves. Mia is usually more flighty when it comes to questionable social situations, and Jill's learned to trust her friend's intuition. The insolent bartender approaches the table, he passes out three glasses of beer. The adult beverages break down the last layer of defense, and with one sip, they feel ready to tell him anything, and let him help them.

"It's okay. I am a police officer in France."

Mia and Jill don't say anything. He catches a sharp stare from Mia and smiles with condescension. He reaches around his back, and in an exaggerated fashion pulls his wallet from his pocket. He flips it open, and a badge flashes out of a clear holder. Mia blinks, then gives Jill an expressive look. Jill stares at the badge, then back at Mia. The man shakes his head smiling.

"You are safe with me. It's your lucky night to have found me here. There are bad people out in this area." He wags his finger at the women, scolding them playfully.

This provokes more sips of beer. The drink works its magic, and soon they grow to appreciate the eccentric corner pub.

"Okay, what are you looking for, sweethearts?"

Jill speaks up. "Rue Gu-y-nemer," in an awkward pronunciation. "Umm, 73 Rue."

The aggressive Antonin leans in, "73 Rue Guynemer. Yes I can help you. I know why you are lost now."

This time, the women lean in, they can't even try to predict his explanation.

"My pets, you are on the wrong street. We have two streets with this name, and you want to find the other street." He laughs, before taking a long sip of his foam and amber drink.

"So . . . you are saying; there are two streets in Paris with the same name, and we are on the wrong street?" Mia wants to straighten the facts thoroughly in her head.

"Yes my American cheese, the street you want to be on is on the other side of the city." He smiles, and waits for the information to settle into their minds a bit.

"What?" Mia exclaims with horror.

"How far?" Jill asks with agitation. She's beginning to doubt Antonin's honesty. She can tell he's drunk. Policeman or not, she senses trouble. Antonin studies the heartened reaction from the women. He pitches back in his chair, folding his arms across his chest in a surly fashion.

"No cheeses, you don't worry. I will take you to your hostel myself. Everything will be fine. The only thing you have to think about now, is finishing your beer. Antonin will handle everything."

Mia catches the bartender looking up from his bar, still arranging his glasses. He looks amused. Was he smiling because of Antonin? But, why? She folds her arms across her chest, resigning to the fact she can't crack the bartender's code. She turns to Jill, the only one that remotely makes sense to her.

"How much do you think a cab ride across Paris will cost?" Mia asks Jill, just before tilting back her glass to get the last big gulp of beer. Mia notices the empty glass causes Antonin to inch closer, he seems inspired by her ruthless drinking. He lights a cigarette.

"Oh Mia, don't be silly. I will take you and pay for your cab. I told you, you don't have to worry about anything now. I'm an officer, and wouldn't feel right if I didn't make sure you got to your hostel safely."

Between the beer and the free cab ride, Mia can't help but smile for him. They are on their way to a bed, and Antonin, the off duty police officer, will escort them there. The smile is persuasive enough for Antonin to prove how helpful he can be, by not lingering, but getting them directly to their hostel. He stands up, then offers his arm to Jill, gesturing for her to rise with him. Jill tucks her arm into his, and reaches to his opposite side to lift her pack. "No, Madame, what are you doing? I'll get that. Please put it down."

Jill drops the bag and giggles.

Antonin extends his hand to Mia, and she playfully rises from her chair, squeezing his hand until she takes a spot next to Jill. There's a slight moment of satisfaction for Antonin. He gently releases himself from their arms, and gives them a French style head tilt, before turning to collect the second pack. The women stand back and watch their officer try to lift both packs. In his best attempt to display his brute strength, he lifts them. It takes him three tries to successfully balance both packs on his shoulders and back. He shouts something in French to the bartender, then points to the door.

Mia goes first, and holds the door open for him. It takes ten steps to reach the corner in front of the pub. Antonin drops the bags and scans the village square. In less than a minute, a bright white cab pulls up to the curb. The trunk instantly pops open. Antonin goes around to the driver's window, he has a short conversation, then loads the packs into the trunk. He walks back to the curb and opens the door for Jill. Mia slides in, and then Antonin. This silences the women. They didn't realize he would be riding with them. They assumed he'd arrange a drop off with the driver, then go back into the bar. They didn't even see him pay for the drinks. A daring stillness takes control of the car. The only movement is the rotating of the steering wheel. Mia decides, it doesn't matter, they are going to the hostel. Jill decides, this might be suspicious, and hopes they were going to the hostel. The driver seems like a legitimate cab driver, and they're thankful he's with them. At a slow twenty-five miles per hour, the cab carries the three random passengers through slanted streets. True to his word, the hostel is at the opposite side of the great dark city. Jill notices that Antonin has his hand on Mia's knee, and is moving it closer to her thigh. He whispers something in her ear, and she fakes a helpless giggle. The car rolls to a stop along a high curb.

"Here you are, the Round World Hostel." The driver shifts into park, then pops the trunk lid open. Everyone in the car turns to get their first glimpse of the hostel. The place is a slim, tall building. There are no windows on the ground floor, but there is a big steel door with an iron security gate. The women spill out of the car on Jill's side. By the time they reach the trunk, Antonin has met them. He's standing in a predatory fashion between them and their hostel. He lifts their packs, but doesn't let go of them.

"Thank you so much, Antonin." Mia says, standing in front of Jill with a protective stance.

Jill slumps back a little, unsure of her role.

"Wait, can I come up with you for a while?" He holds onto Mia's pack tightly. Mia doesn't try to grab it.

"My mom made reservations for just us, but I'll go in and ask if you can."

Antonin's teeth come out. "I don't believe you."

"Here, How about I give you my phone number, and that way you know I'm not ditching you."

The bullish French man passes a pack to Jill, then pulls his own phone from his back pocket, passing it to Mia. She enters her number into his phone. He takes it back, and presses the call button. Her phone rings in her back pocket, and Antonin smiles. He hands her the pack and pushes himself up against her. She steps back, focused on making a clean break from the officer.

"I want you to have this." He places an object into Mia's hand.

"I can't take this!"

"It's okay, I want you to know I'm serious about you."

Then, good luck befall the women. The front light above the hostel door clicks on, and the big iron door swings open. The most handsome man is standing in the door frame, waving to Mia and Jill. Before they even say a goodbye, both women make a desperate dash for the door, straight to the warmth and protection of the really good looking guy and the hostel.

"Are you Mia?" He asks, in a husky Australian accent. Mia nods, hypnotized by the charm and masculinity of her rescue hero. He leans in close, whispering in her ear; "Do you want me to get rid of that guy?" He nods at the man, who's negotiating with the cab driver to wait for him while he tries to come inside with the women.

Mia nods again.

"Okay, come in quick. I'll take care of him." He gestures to Mia and Jill to step in further, out of sight from the entrance. He pulls shut the security gate and the big door.

He turns and gives the women a bright smile. "You two look like you've had quite the night. I'm glad you made it. I almost gave up on you. I've been waiting up. Mia your mom called about an hour ago. She just wants to make sure you made it here safely."

Mia blushes. Suddenly several pounding knocks on the door interrupt the peaceful vibe. The Australian hostel manager laughs. "There's your friend."

"He said he was a policeman. He said he was going to help us, but, look, he gave me his badge." Mia wants to purge herself of the confusing predicament, and defend her good reputation to the Australian in Paris who gives sanctuary. She grows quiet, realizing her tone is overly excited. She tries to shift down.

The Australian takes the badge momentarily, before handing it back to her. "You have to be careful out there."

"I know it's fake." Mia answers bashfully.

"What a weirdo." The Australian laughs again.

He turns to open the door, while using his other hand to communicate to Mia and Jill to stand off to the side out of sight.

"Hello mate, what can I do for you?"

In an irritated voice, Antonin replies: "I need to talk to those girls. Just for a minute. I need to come in."

"Oh, friend, I'm sorry, but this is a reservation only hostel. I can't let you in." Antonin tries to peer into the foyer of the hostel, but the Australian has the door opened only a few inches. "I'm sorry, the ladies have gone to bed."

"My taxi's left. I just need to come in to call a new taxi." Antonin argues, exiled behind the bars of the security door.

"I can call for you, but I can't let you in. Do you want me to call?" The Australian maintains a relaxed vibe, while waiting for the fake officer to give up. Antonin frowns at the hostel manager, then walks off into the darkness.

The Australian locks the doors shut. "Hmm, that was interesting. You said he told you he was an officer?"

"Yes." Mia's still flustered from the intense confrontation with Antonin.

"So, you two are going to be in room 3E, it's just upstairs and down to the end of the hall on your right. There are two beds waiting for you. I'm going to bed now. I stayed up past my bedtime waiting on you two." He yawns, and turns to disappear around a corner in the downstairs.

"Thank you!" Jill calls out.

Mia and Jill find their beds, and are delighted to discover the room is luxuriously theirs alone. A jolt of sound breaks their moment. The shrill ring of Mia's phone in her back pocket cuts the happy mood. Jill rushes to shut the door, trying to muffle the sound, and not wake anyone who may be sleeping in a nearby room. Mia grabs the phone.

"It's him!" She whispers, holding the phone away from her like it's a venomous snake. She settles herself, and presses the silence button on the side of the phone. Then she stares at the badge, which she's been holding since she showed it to the Aussie downstairs. "Is it real?" she asks, pressing it tightly between her fingers. She passes it to Jill.

"I don't know," Jill answers, turning the badge in the moonlight that filters through the small bedroom. She lowers, then lifts her hand to sense the weight. Jill shakes her head and passes it back to Mia.

"I'm keeping it," Mia sighs, and tucks the memento back into her backpack. On point, her phone begins to buzz and vibrate. She grabs the phone and shuts the power off, before sliding it back into her pants pocket. Before Mia can say goodnight to Jill, who's already wriggling down into her sleeping bag, a loud shout drifts up to their second floor window. Jill pauses and looks at Mia. "Did you hear that?"

"Mia!" A spectral voice cries from the street below.

"Oh, God, it's Antonin." Mia cowers into the corner of her bed, paralyzed from the aggressive pursuit of an insane French man.

"Mia." His voice echoes through the still night, giving both women goose bumps.

"What should we do?" Mia asks.

"Don't go to that window! I don't want him to see us. I think we should just try to go to sleep," Jill says with genuine support.

Mia doesn't answer, she simply wiggles down into her flannel-lined sleeping bag and closes her eyes. Jill closes her eyes, too. Together they lie in new beds, listening to the brazen shouts from a man on the street, who in their best judgment, discerns, is not a police officer.

Neuf

Jill wakes first. She rises out of bed in confusion. Not knowing where she is for the first nano-second of consciousness. She's caught between a dream and the plain reality of the hostel room. It isn't until she sees Mia, folded up into quarters, tucked down deep inside a sleeping bag; that she's able to recall where she is and how she happens to be in this place. She rubs her dry eyes and sniffs to loosen the dust that's collected in her nose. She pulls her knees up, then kicks off the rest of her sleeping bag. She takes an inventory of herself: black ankle socks, blue yoga pants, an over-stretched sports bra, and a faded grey sweatshirt. Her hair is still pulled back into a loose bun from the night before. She decides she needs to figure out a proper outfit for the day, and she has to work with the limited wardrobe she's been carrying on her back all this time. She doesn't want to wear the same things she had worn during their last time spent in Paris. She figures she owes Paris better than that. On heavy, slow tiptoes, she creeps over to her bag. She tries not to breathe while creeping past her tired sleeping friend. She unzips the main compartment, and starts to fish out all the clothes she thinks might qualify. Now that she's been touring Paris, she has a better idea of what she might wear. She finds a pair of charcoal black tights, her black heels, and a long green skirt. For the top, she selects the wool sweater she wore almost every day in Zermatt. She smells it. She could get away with one more day in it. Last week she purchased a light green patterned scarf from a street vendor. She pulls it out, and decides to wear it. Proud of her new look, she lays her outfit on her bed. She grabs her cosmetic bag and tiptoes out of the room to track down a bathroom. Jill revels in these few minutes that she has to herself. She doesn't feel obligated to wake up and visit about nothing right away.

By the time Jill returns to the room, Mia's awake.

"Good morning sunshine," Mia's ecstatic. She has all her clothes spread out on her bed, trying to reorganize her pack, and like Jill, she picks out a fresh new look from old stinky clothes. Jill can read Mia like a book when she happens to be in this particular mood. She doesn't have to say it. Jill can tell she's giddy in the anticipation of a reunion with her Irish crush. This is fine, Jill's equally inspired by the prospect of touring Paris alone for the day.

"I can't believe it, Jill, you're actually flying home in two days! You know, you can skip your flight and come to Spain with me." Mia folds a few tops and winks at Jill.

"It's okay. I'm not sad about it. I've been feeling kind of homesick. Plus, I'm pretty satisfied with all the things we've seen on this trip. I'm really pumped to get to spend the whole day in Paris. It's exactly what I want"

"What are you going to do?" Mia stops packing, truly concerned about her friend's plan. They've been looking after each other the whole time, and Mia can't' help but feel a little protective of Jill.

Jill smiles peacefully. "I want to go back to the Louvre. I could spend the whole day just hanging out with Da Vinci and Monet." Jill's eyes start to glaze over as she romanticizes getting up close and personal with some of the world's greatest art. "I also want to try to see some more cathedrals. There as so many. I might just take a good walk around the city. Try to shop a little more. I definitely came in under my travel budget, so I have some extra money to play with." Jill loses focus, thinking about the possibilities of her day.

Mia's voice changes, she's serious. "Tonight . . . are you going to go out?"

"No, I'll come back before night fall. Have a quiet night. I'll hang out in bed or on the internet."

"Good." Mia leans back, glad to hear her friend would be safe today. "So, tomorrow you'll grab the first train back to Amsterdam?"

"For sure! I'm the one who should be worried about you. That Amsterdam train depot is tricky. Right when you get outside, and have to find the right bus . . . When I think of all the difficulties and crazy stress we've had on our trip, the central train-bus-station place in Amsterdam is still my least favorite!" Jill sighs.

Mia answers, "Zeeburg, the bus says the name right on the side." She snatches her shampoo, soap, conditioner and leaves.

Once alone, Jill drops her towel and starts to dress. She looks great. Even though there are no mirrors; she's confident, she's rocking a strong look. She tied her hair into two braided buns fastened tightly to each side of her head. This isn't a Paris look, but she wants to make sure she represents a little California in her travels today. She decides she looks smart.

After more rearranging, Mia and Jill make their way down the narrow stairs of the secure hostel. The room at the bottom of the stairs has a couch and a television. Four people are hanging out, watching the morning news. They turn and give a light greeting, before giving their attention back to the television. They explore the kitchen, and Jill looks longingly through the foyer at the room with the computers set up for internet use. There isn't any food, but they help themselves to some complimentary black tea sipped from styrofoam cups. Soon they find themselves embarking on another journey, out into the bustle of the day, tracking their way to the metro stop. Up one street, and around another, they find their metro station.

"Can you remember this, Jill? This is your station, and that's how you have to get back."

Jill rolls her eyes. "I'll be fine, let's get you to your train."

Mia pauses, just watching her friend for a moment, wanting reassurance that she'll be okay. She loves Jill, and has first- hand knowledge how deceptive this unfamiliar city can be.

"Really, Mia, I'm going to be fine, and will see you tomorrow."

Mia's thoughts roam, she finds them leading to what the day brings, and the day brings Paul. They continue onto the metro. Surprised at how quickly the transfer occurs, fifteen minutes later, they're standing in the Nord train depot, preparing to say goodbye. Mia's train is already in the station and travelers are boarding. The separation is solidified in this exchange of parting words. They aren't prepared, hadn't even realized, that leaving the other would feel so difficult and objectionable. Mia feels emotion, and sick worry, and accountable for leaving her good friend alone in an entirely different country. She shoves down her issues, deep into her guts. She hooks her fingers firmly around the straps of her pack. Jill stands quiet, examining the indent of her toe showing through her left maryjane. No words can help, no words can properly explain this troubling ache that they don't know what to do with. So, it needs to be simple. Mia reaches out and gives Jill a quick, hard hug. Jill hugs back. Upon releasing, Mia turns and starts to walk away. "I'll see you tomorrow then. Remember the Zeeburg bus!"

Jill gazes with eyes wide open, she could always count on her friend to cowgirl up, riding off into the sunset, hitting the trail and finding the good fortune on the other side. She raises her voice, to make sure it carries to her friend's ears, "Give the boys my best!"

Jill remains, the solace of the departure ripples through her, and she lets the weight of her body settle into the ground she stands on. She hangs her shoulders and relaxes her posture. Even though Mia has climbed aboard the train, Jill wants to wait, to watch it pull away. She thinks it's the right thing to do. As she stands, she questions the confusion behind their sad goodbye. Why were they so affected by this? Then a slight distraction, she reaches down, sliding her fingers along her waist until she can make out the outline of her tights that have been creeping down, halfway down her hip. She digs her fingers under the elastic through the skirt, and hoists them up. The train has gone.

Jill turns and walks over to the concession. She buys a café au lait, smelling the dark roasted beans as she sips, wrapping her cool hands around the cup to feel the warmth. The day is hers, all hers. She sits on a bench, deciding to simply enjoy the coffee while deciding what she truly wants to do. When she stands up, again her tights have inched their way down, and are closer to her thighs than her waist. "*This will not do,*" she tells herself in an exaggerated English accent; she narrates in her head. Even though she's in Paris, she wants to pretend she's mysterious and English. She's having her own fantasy, and reality doesn't have to interfere with her strange imagination.

Creeping tights make her feel English. Her issue immediately cheers her up, and she's forgotten all about abandoning her friend for Paris. She stays for a second, trying to discreetly tug her tights back up. She considers the problem, relating to her own scenario. With all the walking she plans on doing, the last thing she wants is to find herself standing in front of the Mona Lisa completely distracted by slippery tights. She reviews her options: she could take them off, except she hasn't shaved her legs since her first day in Zermatt. She could go back to the hostel and change into pants, but that would take over an hour. She could readjust, put her underwear over her tights, to hold them in place, or she could just keep trying to cinch them up with her fingers all day. Jill opts for the third choice: putting her underwear on over her tights. "This is brilliant she thinks(in an English accent)," she skips over to the women's bathroom.

Pulling and tugging, she finally shimmies herself back into the charcoal colored tights. Tucked within the protection of the ladies restroom stall she looks down to examine her new wardrobe situation. The hot pink silk panties certainly do stand out from the rest of the ensemble. The vibrant hue is almost electric in contrast to her dark earth tones. The vision makes her laugh, and a new thought enters her mind, *"Now, I'm like a super hero, with my panties on the outside of my tights! Super Hero Jill, roaming the streets of Paris, fearless and impervious to cultural conditioning!"* She releases her skirt, it hangs back down past her knees. She takes a few steps in place, then a few hops to admire and test her handy work. The panties are working perfectly. The tights are sliding nowhere!

Two minutes later, Jill exits the bathroom, beaming and ready to embark on her solo adventure. She already feels lighter and free. Her bulky cameras dangling and knocking about from her neck, she even takes her travelers pocket from underneath the shell of her sweater, sporting it as an accessory. She can wear her functional items any way she wants now that Mia isn't around to feel uneasy. Once out onto the streets of Paris, imagination permeates into her heart.

Despite the flighty sensation of navigating and deciding for herself, she walks down the street as if she owns it. This is her day, her experience, and she is going to take this gift. Her thoughts carry her to a deeper level; "In the end, when it's all said and done, we will all look back on our lives and remember them in moments. The moments are what mark the transcendence along our paths on these human experiences. This time that I have now, here in Paris, can and should be one of those moments. It's up to me, my responsibility to make this time mean something. I've only been here in this world a short twenty-four years, but all the years and all of the choices and connections have lead up to today, in this time. I can use what I know, and try to understand what I don't, and as this day unfolds, I will be a better person for having had this experience." Jill's personal pep talk pushes her down the sidewalk further, and true to her love, she decides to go where her heart wishes. Back to the Louvre.

. . . . .

This visit to the museum of all museums feels different. She's never actually spent time in a museum alone before. There isn't anyone to discuss what she sees, or to say "look at this one!" This observation of art creates a more intimate and soulful experience. Somehow the figures and images become internalized. She spends close to an hour, meditating and losing herself in an ancient Byzantine mosaic. She walks down lonely halls, away from the more popular streams of traffic. She peers into them deeply, and relaxes her eyes to let the colors mesh and soften. One piece provokes tears, and another causes her to turn away.

Time evades her. Jill finds herself standing near a group, appreciating a dark impressionist painting when she feels something tickle her thigh. The sensation pulls her from her thoughts and she flinches. She senses a faint brush on her leg a second time, then she realizes what it might be. She gulps, and can feel a gentle pat on the top of her maryjane shoes. She looks down, and, there, around her ankles, hot pink contrasts against her charcoal black tights. Before she can even pick them up, she has to do one thing. This is pure instinct. She has to look around the grand room to see who else has caught her with her panties around her ankles, over the outside of her tights. She sees them, the faces, looking as confused and stunned as she is. So she drops, squatting and grabbing, then pulling them up, but trying to do it while navigating under her skirt, in an attempt to not reveal any more. Like wildfire, the interest spreads. First two people notice, then three people notice the first two noticing something. Then other people direct their attention from the painting to the animated woman hitching up her drawers directly beneath a great masterpiece.

The hot pink panties are back in place and Jill's standing up again, facing the confused crowd. People go to art galleries to see things that will make them think, but, what they didn't expect to find that day, was a clumsy American woman who wears her underwear on the outside of her clothes, only to lose them around her ankles in a room full of people. In an interesting way, Jill did make them think. For one instant in the Louvre that day, the mellow art vibe had been assaulted and interrupted by a crazy tourist with too many cameras around her neck, and clothes that don't seem to fit right. Jill turns and faces the wall, like a serpent doing her best to slink out of the room. She's not compelled to apologize to anyone, they would understand. The best she can do is to just leave, find a bathroom, and put the hot pink panties back on the inside of her tights. Unfortunately, she isn't lucky enough to make an easy escape. Before turning to leave the grand room, a security guard who's been standing opposite Jill, catches her eye. She's stuck. By his expression, she can tell that he's been watching the whole event. She could die, but instead; gives him a hopeless smile. Jill speed walks through the halls of powerful imagery with an apologetic walk, holding tight to the band of her panties. She no longer feels elevated or distinguished, even the English accent has abandoned her.

She back tracks all the way to the entrance before finding a bathroom. She rushes in, and locks herself in a modern stall. She collapses to the toilet, and before her entire weight has settled, the tears start to pour. They're hot tears, on hot cheeks, red from embarrassment. She has to hold her breath, so that she doesn't let out loud whimpers for strangers to hear. As she sits, so small, so American, she's overcome by everything at once. All the humiliation of the trip, potato dinners, jolted cameras, scaring teenage boys who ride the metro, assaulting teenage girls who ride the Amsterdam bus system, farting in one's sleep, and now this. She's humiliated, and it hurts. It hurts so bad, to do so much harm without intention. She starts to believe that she's just faulty, a dysfunction of a person. How can she be so awkward? How can she love herself, when today she doesn't even like herself? She lets the tears come, because she doesn't know what else to do. The crying isn't stopping or easing. A quarter hour has passed. She realizes she has probably needed to cry many times on the trip but couldn't. Now that she's alone, her heart takes over, twisting and purging so many incomprehensible moments. Eventually the tears run low, and the oozing from her nose regresses to sniffles. She's gone through half the roll of toilet paper. Wiping and smoothing out the creases of unhappiness. What a comfort and practical commodity tissue paper is. She thinks about her relationship with toilet paper, as she sits in a pitiful slump, hidden with the toilets of the Louvre. She balls some of the tissue paper up, and stuffs it down into her travel pocket. Thoughts of toilet paper and traveler's pockets lighten her mood, and prepare her to move on. After all, she can't spend her entire day in Paris, hiding in a public toilet.

Once out of the bathroom, with the underwear back on the inside of her tights, she takes to the streets of Paris to track down some lunch and regroup. The best thing to do is to pretend that never happened. After all, she's in France, and no one needs to know!

Jill passes three modest looking café's, but she keeps going. She needs to put some miles between herself and the Louvre. She can't help but feel disappointed that she defiled a place she considers to be favored by God himself. With each step away from her art fetish, she feels a little better. Her thoughts move to a forward position, right behind her eyes, and she studies the direction her feet carry her. The neighborhood includes a small shopping district. She slows down to study the fruit outside of a produce shop. Bunches of spinach are wilted and the potatoes are aged. Seeing the worn, bruised vegetables makes her miss California. Back home, she could just walk up to a tree or a bush and pick food off of it. Fresh, sweet food, that gives texture and culture to average meals.

It isn't the discovery of the perfect lunch spot that stops her, it's her hunger. Jill walks into a small ice cream parlor. She can't speak much French, but she's managed to learn how to ask for chocolate with expertise. To Jill, chocolate is universal, and no language can keep her from her addiction. She steps up to the counter. She can tell by the expression on the cashiers face that she knows Jill's American. Jill smiles, the short-haired girl smiles back.

"Un café glacee?" Even though she's giving a request, it still sounds like a question.

Just like the sweetness of the ice cream, the girl acknowledges with a formalized version of kindness. Within minutes, Jill is holding a fresh frozen chocolate drizzled coffee, melting into the shape of the paper cup. With her ice cream in hand, she walks over to a towering cathedral. She doesn't know the name of the church, but as she approaches, she can see it's locked up. Many people are using the steps for a place to sit and eat lunch or smoke a cigarette while watching pigeons converse. Jill sits, too.

She sits on the stone steps, and watches the world pass by her. She sees the people moving and going. Her eyes follow the lines of the cathedral point up to the heavens. She watches lovers caress and sneak their hands in places that make her blush. At first she is in the present, embracing the act of sitting and learning, but then she feels stuck. Stuck right there on the stone steps, afraid to move, not knowing where to go. She thought of tomorrow and of the Irishmen. Why is she so reluctant to go see them? They got along well enough. They were all completely sweet to her. The only person who even remotely hurt her feelings was the American from Wisconsin who shunned her to sleep in his tent alone. But, even that, wasn't personal or meant to insult her. She feels regret, because she's wasting time thinking on the Irishmen.

Jill works hard to organize her thoughts. The Louvre, ice cream, relaxing beneath a Cathedral with an unknown name, and now . . . what to do? In many ways, this day is the last day of her trip. Tomorrow would be spent traveling back to Amsterdam as well as preparing to board her plane early the next morning. This is her day to go nowhere, and be nowhere, just to take France and as many experiences that are offered her way. She wants to take enough of it, so that she can keep it with her, always. She wants to revisit these events and places, to think about how humble and objectionable her life might seem, since she now has something to compare her world and culture too. *"This place must be the food and art capital of the world,"* she concludes, after scooping the last bite of runny ice cream into her mouth.

She walks some more, every now and then stopping to photograph the corner of a gothic structure, or a fountain. She finds a small market, and wanders around for close to forty five minutes. She studies the way the food looks as it sits on shelves and displays in cases. She considers dinner, and the setting sun, she thinks of Mia, and how dinner will feel a little lonely tonight.

With a twenty four inch baguette and a bottle of ten euro wine, Jill boards the metro to head back to the hostel. Safely secured in her room, she examines her options. She promised Mia she would stay inside when it got dark, and she's now so close to going home to California safely, the last thing she wants is to run into trouble. The word "trouble" has a suggestion attached to it. The word tempts her. That's when she pulls out her wine key which is part of the Swiss army knife she purchased at a Zermatt gift shop. Using it for the first time, alone, and in Paris . . . *"how appropriate,"* she thinks. She grabs a paper cup from downstairs, and fills it halfway with wine. She feels like a failure, sitting alone in her room with a cup of vino in hand. She sips it, the paper gives the wine a displeasing aftertaste.

"This won't do," Her English accent interrupts the sad affair. *"Well, get up then. Don't dilly delly."* She sighs, disturbed that the absence of her friend has somehow been replaced by an imaginary English accent. Soon, Jill's back downstairs, standing on the street curb where they had been delivered by the fake officer. She sneers at the spot where the cab was parked, then raises her bottle of wine up to her lips. She drinks.

She imagines how she might look, standing alone on the sidewalk, a big bottle of French wine dangling from her right hand, a weird travel pocket double wrapped around her neck. She decides she'd look more natural, if she walked. So she does. She walks around the block, and empties half the bottle of red. She feels tipsy, and the nightscape is starting to glimmer and beckon her to explore. She stops and holds up a finger, wagging it at the horizon. She smiles at Paris. Then turns, dropping the half-drunk bottle in a nearby trashcan. She begins the walk back to her room, lonely for the bottle and for Mia, and for California. Two men pass by her. They wave. Jill waves back.

"He-lo" the young man with a distinct accent greets her. The man next to him tips his head in approval at her, adjusting his NBA basketball hat.

"Good evening." Jill slurs, feeling social and free.

"You are American?" The first man inquires.

"Yes. Where are you from?"

"We are Ukrainian. You know? I like your neck ornament. Is like the Flavor-Flav?"

"Ummm, yes. It's my traveler's pocket, I don't go anywhere without it."

"Oh, yeah? You are like Michael Jackson with his white glove? It is your thing, yes?" He gives her two standing thumbs up, approving of her unique style.

Jill laughs hysterically, and nods her head. For a moment she entertains the possibility of joining the two strange foreign boys who are out to enjoy Paris, while simultaneously considering her resemblance to Flavor-Flav. Sadly enough, she considers the value and utility of wearing a clock around her neck, imagining how it would fit beside her cameras and travel pocket, deciding if she would prefer to set it to time back home, or abroad.

The friend in the NBA hat asks, "Are you staying at the hostel?"

"Yes. You both are staying there too?" Jill is pleased to be conversing with potential friends. Then, her buzz pulls her back a bit. "Well, I'm heading back. Have a good night, then!"

"You too, Flavorful Miss!" The men continue, walking in the opposite direction as Jill.

She's entirely inspired by her cool new nickname, and decides she can't wait to tell Mia. The Flavorful Miss walks on, with a grateful and enlightened smile.

The rest of the night passes quietly, and in the morning she boards a train.

Dix

Jill pulls her travel pouch out from under her sweatshirt. She tugs and pulls on the slack of the flesh colored cord. Once she has the pouch section in her hand, she unzips the oversized hanging wallet and pulls out her passport and boarding pass. She's now ready, wearing her lucky sweatshirt to ensure safe passage. There would be a brief stop in Brussels before reaching Amsterdam. She skips over breakfast and realizes she would have to purchase some of the weird train food from the lady with the cart. She's craving Pepsi. Today her cameras are packed away in her bag. She decides she's done taking pictures. Tonight she plans on drinking, and drinking a lot, but not too much that she would oversleep and miss her morning flight back to the states. She just wants to drown out the sadness and the awkwardness among the men, and the hard goodbye to Mia. She wants to drink so that she won't feel it all. It will be too much. She never liked the ending of a journey, it was always so melancholy and final.

The train moves with swiftness, pulling her away from Paris, rushing to the Netherlands. She's caught someplace in between. The place between the coming and the going. She's a passenger, and can do nothing but exist in a state of locomotion. She looks out the window and lets her thoughts go. They were in between, too.

. . . . .

Four hours and two empty Pepsi cans later, Jill's train is pulling into the Amsterdam station. She's giddy to have made it and wonders if Mia experienced a similar burst of joy when she accomplished the same victory yesterday. Having found her way back earns her the confidence to climb aboard the Zeeburg bus with little to no doubt. Soon, she's boldly standing at the corner up the road from the campground bent forward from the weight of her cumbersome pack. It will feel good to take it off and know that she doesn't have to put it back on until tomorrow morning.

Back in Paris this morning, when she was alone she wanted to wear her jeans and sweatshirt, but now that she's about to join friends, she second guesses her attire. The jeans will probably annoy Mia, but at least the cameras are packed away. One foot after the other she walks down the sidewalk that takes her to camp. This last quarter mile of the day's travels prove to be the most difficult and the closer she gets to the Irishmen, the more hesitant and reluctant she becomes. She even debates stopping in the middle of the sidewalk to dig through her pack and apply fresh makeup. She shakes herself out of her compulsive anxiousness and turns down the path that leads to the camp.

She arrives, walking right past the registration office and over to one of the picnic tables in the courtyard. Caught unprepared, she's surprised to discover a welcoming party.

"There she is! Our brilliant lass! We've been waiting for you." Mickey shouts in his knee-weakening Irish cadence.

Jill turns to look behind her, disbelieving that they're cheering for her. She reasons they must see someone else. There's too much affection and joy. She's sure they are mistaken, or she's mistaken.

"There's my girl! I missed you, Jill!" Mickey says. He walks over to her and stretches his arm out to bring Jill into a loving hug. Jill blushes, feeling him push her face into his soft thick sweater. "I was feeling worried about you. How was your trip, my love?"

"Uh, me?" Jill's squeaks.

"Stop bogarting my sweetheart!" Sean pushes Mickey away and pulls Jill to him. He gracefully leads her by the hand over to the table. He lifts her pack for her and gently escorts Jill to a place on the bench he's chosen especially for her. Before she's even settled into the spot, a bottle of Heineken has been set in front of her. She's sandwiched in between the most charming green eyed men she'll ever hope to meet. She's completely overwhelmed. Like a deer trapped in a storm of headlights, Jill freezes. Unsure of what to say, or even how to look. She's worried it's a cruel joke, that they might be playing a game with her. But as they speak, explaining and remaining kind, she grows to accept that maybe they might be sincere. The irresistible charm radiates from their smiles and washes away all of Jill's reservations.

Jill holds tight to her composure, "Where's Mia?"

"Oh, I see how it is then. We've been sitting here waiting for you for the last three hours, and all you want to know is where Mia is. You just saw her the other day. You haven't seen me in ten days!" Mickey complains.

Jill's confused. She didn't expect Sean or Mickey to have such an attachment to her. "Thanks for waiting for me," she answers.

"Mia went to a brewery tour with Paul and Addison, but she didn't want you to come here and not find anyone. She asked us to hang out and wait for you. She'll be back pretty soon." Mickey says. He pushes the beer an inch closer to her suggestively.

Sitting next to the men makes her jumpy. She's sure they are flirting with her, but the flirting just doesn't make sense. She considers all far-fetched scenarios. Perhaps her crush on Mickey was transparent, and Mia could tell the entire time. Did Mia tell the men she has a crush on them? Maybe Mickey heard how she's been traveling alone and finds it impressive and attractive. Perhaps he thought she was a dumb tourist before, but now she somehow earned status in his perspective. She's at a loss and needs to feel out the unexpected situation.

In the meantime, the attention from Mickey is nothing to grumble about. His accent, his green eyes, and his bullish character make her dizzy with adoration. She takes a minute to look at him. He enjoys this. He has on a tight white shirt and a blue cabled sweater which drapes over his physique unzipped. The white of his shirt causes the white of his eyes to sparkle, and if she isn't careful, creates a hypnotic effect. The only thing to do, is to talk to Sean!

"Sean, it's so good to see you. The last time I saw you was the night we went to the redlight district."

Sean looks away embarrassed. "I don't know what happened that night. I think I was drugged." When he answers, she can hear his agitation, recalling the dangerous evening.

"You and I were stuck together most of the night. Thanks for staying close by me. I was a little scared that night." Jill takes a sip of her beer.

"Not at all. I'm glad to accompany you. Happy to protect my sweet lass. I'd do it again in a heartbeat." He sucks in his gut and puffs out his chest slightly.

Jill visualizes the image of Sean, teasing the girls in the windows, making them spin and bend over for him. It amuses her that today he's bragging about being some gallant protector.

Jill keeps looking over her shoulder, expecting to see Mia and her redheaded entourage coming down the hill. Any other scenario, she'd be thrilled to have this time with the handsome Irish men along with the familiar way they flatter her. They're as charming as ever, but this time she seems to be an object of interest here at the Zeeburg campground. What changed? She can't figure it out. Jill squirms under the heat of the attention from Mickey and Sean who are sitting on either side of her, grinning, and trying to look seductive. The sun is shining bright and the picnic table is warm and good. The perfect place to find herself caught between men who seem to think she's extremely appealing.

"Other than waiting for you here at camp today, there is something else Mia asked us to do." Mickey inches away from Jill on the bench, and leans back, resting his elbow on the table top. He looks smug and enjoys seeing Jill's interest spike with the mystery favor. She can't trust this situation. It doesn't make sense and her connection to Mia is the only thing that feels real to her. Mickey just sits back, watching her, not giving away the information. Sean is looking at her as well, with a sly smile curling the corners of his lips.

"What did she ask? Does it have to do with me?" Jill can tell it has to do with her because of the intent expression both men are sporting. She isn't used to men staring at her this way and it makes her want to go retreat into the women's bathroom until Mia comes back. Instead, she tries the next best thing: drink her beer.

"Addison's travel companion moved into camp last week. Her name is Amy. Mia is sleeping in Paul and Thomas's tent. So, she asked if you could squeeze in with us. In our tent."

Jill's eyes fail to blink, considering the two nuggets of information that have just been dropped into her lap. Her eyebrow arches as she realizes Mia's been sleeping in a tent with both Paul and Thomas. She wonders how the arrangement works. Did Mia get the time with Paul she had hoped for, or did something else take place last night? But more than thinking of Mia's night, Jill is dumbstruck by the fate of her own. She's being invited to sleep in a tent next to Mickey. In her wildest dreams she never would have imagined this morning, . . . that by this evening, she'd be in a tent next to an attractive Irishman who she secretly harbors an impossible crush for.

Yet right now he can't take his eyes off her. Still, she doubts all his sincerity. All Jill can grasp for in her nervousness is that she needs Mia. Too much information and strange vibes leave her perplexed. So perplexed, that there's no room for any other feeling. In seven long sips, she finishes her beer. Before she even sets the empty can on the picnic table, Sean places a brand new one in front of Jill. He winks. Then opens another one for himself. Jill wishes to be invisible. In her mind she takes inventory of what had changed between now and when she left all those days ago. Do they like her now because they plan on taking her back to their tent tonight? That's a strong probability. Do they like her now because she hasn't tried to flirt or pursue them and they find that challenging? Or, perhaps they like the way she stayed in Paris to do her own thing. She lost close to ten pounds over the course of the trip. Could it be this weight loss is enough to make her look really hot?" She slides her white sunglasses down over her eyes and resigns to the fact that she can't analyze this one.

"That's so nice of you guys. Are you sure it's okay that I stay in your tent with you?"

"Okay? . . . Jill, I've been waiting for you all afternoon! We're happy to have you sleep with us tonight." Mickey gives Sean a twisted look, and then turns to Jill and winks. Jill's face flushes and she's glad for her sunglasses. She can't grip why their invitation is presented in such a teasing fashion.

The trio drops the topic of conversation. They pass the hour sitting in the sun, telling stories and finishing what's left of the stack of vending machine beer bottles. The two bottles sitting in front of Jill have the labels peeled back by her timid, busy fingers. Mickey reaches out and decides to tell her a story to try to help her feel comfortable.

"We're headed back to Ireland at the end of the month, too."

"Are you happy to go back home? I'm so homesick." Jill responds, grateful to talk of pleasant things.

"No, I'm so irate about having to go back home. Sean and I have been here almost six months. We have to head back because our Visas are requiring us to. That, and we've run out of money." He gives her a sad smile.

"Oh, I'm sorry. You know, you should come visit the United States. You would love it. I could show you guys San Francisco or Yosemite!" Jill offers, fantasizing about getting to play tour guide to her Irish Charms.

"Yeah, well, we never really wanted to go to the U.S." Sean answers, humored by Jill's assumption. This momentarily disturbs Jill. America is incredible, she fully believes everyone wants to go there. It's hurtful to think they don't appreciate her homeland. She shifts her direction away from Sean and focuses on Mickey as a form of protest against Sean's lack of passion for her country.

"You could come to Ireland, Jill. You can live with me at my house and help work our farm this summer," Mickey suggests.

Jill starts to laugh nervously. Did this alluring, well -traveled Irish man just invite her to live with him?

"I mean it, Jill. I don't want to go back there. I left on bad terms. It would be much better if you were there to hang out with. I have a lot of work to do when I get home." When he says this part, he stares straight into her eyes, casting an intense expression. Jill looks away, focusing on a patch of honeysuckle trailing up the side of the bathroom wall. She tries her best to seem indifferent to his mindful gaze.

Jill pictures a scene in her mind: Mickey sweaty with no shirt on, bailing hay or plowing a field. The rolling green hills choked by romantic coastal fog. Her mind drifts, teased by the thought. How fitting, of course he works on a farm in Ireland. She's like a fish caught in a net, completely consumed by his story. "On what bad terms did you leave?"

"Well, Jill, that's why I left." Mickey stands up and sets his foot on the bench, leaning forward with a manly story-telling kind of stature. His face changes and she can see he's remembering a place of sadness, perhaps heartbreak. "On our family farm, it's just me and my dad. My mom left us a long time ago to live in the city. I had a really beautiful girlfriend who moved in with us. She was great. She would take care of all the household stuff, cooking and cleaning. All my dad and I had to do was focus on the farm work." He pauses, to check in with Jill, and see how caught up she is in his story. He's pleased with her empty, absorbent stare. She waits, fully committed to hear how his bad terms were to play out. "So one day I was coming in for lunch after working all morning in the fields," Mickey looks up at the sky, trying to summon the words to describe what he found. "It was my girlfriend and my dad . . . in bed together. That's why I left."

Jill slides back into the bench, completely affected by the horror of his story. She can't believe how any woman could do that to Mickey. Filled with compassion, she now understands why he doesn't want to return. "But, you want me to go there? You invited me to your farm for the summer? Your dad is there? What happened to the girlfriend?"

In a jaded voice, he replies, "Oh, yeah, we worked it out. She's with my father now. I'm okay with it. I just needed some time to get away from all that."

This final detail of his story of woe knocks Jill sideways. Jill's quiet, she's not sure she knows what to say.

With a speck of paranoia, she thinks she sees a slight hint of a smile between Sean and Mickey. They drop their poker faces for just a second, but Jill catches it. She debates the possibility that this is another one of those blarney stories that they love to tell. What if he made the whole thing up? Does he live on a farm? After spending less than two hours with Sean and Mickey, Jill feels her whole world tilt on its axis. Nothing makes sense, and the beers don't help. Or do they? But then, who cares? She likes his story of the farm, and likes to fantasize about herself existing there with him. She has no clue what Ireland is like, and in her head, its landscape resembles the Ireland of the movies. Jill turns to Sean. "Is this true?"

"Oh yes, every bit of the story is true. That slut, she was no good for Mickey!" He nods solemnly, sorry for his friend's bad fortune.

"Hey, Sean, careful calling her a slut. We're still friends." Mickey says in a lonesome tone.

"Okay, but why did you come to Europe, Sean?" Jill questions. She tries to poke holes in the story.

Sean stretches his arms up over his head. "Why not? I just came along to hang out." The way Sean said this makes it sound so common, as if it's the most natural thing in the world to drift aimlessly in foreign countries for half a year. He speaks of it, like he had simply decided to go out for a bite of pizza or something else equally casual. Jill suspects deceit, which causes her to doubt the heavy flirting and the invitation back to their tent. She also needs to confront herself with the possibility that she might find herself in a tent with Mickey and Sean tonight. How will she handle that situation? She's leaving first thing in the morning, as soon as the sun rises. She has nothing to invest in these relationships. She's almost home, and up to this point, she's made it intact. Her goal is to continue self-preservation. Her goal is to go home.

Finally, her love and rock appears, walking with Thomas and Paul on either side of her. Behind them are Addison and his travel companion Amy. Jill leaps from her spot on the picnic table and scrambles to greet Mia.

Mia reciprocates the warm greeting with a warm hug. It's their last night together, and although they don't speak of this fact, they understand it completely. Jill doesn't want to let go of Mia, she wishes she could just stay in the childish hug, holding on, and dodging her bouts of panic that have been cultivated by the Irishmen.

Mia leans in and whispers, "So, tonight, it's okay if you sleep in Mickey and Sean's tent?" When she pulls back, she looks into Jill's anxious eyes. Jill trusts in Mia. She bows her head in agreement. Whatever the situation is, it doesn't matter now. Jill has Mia, and she can cling to her for the rest of the night.

"Yes. I don't care. I'll sleep in their tent. Thanks for working everything out for me, Mia. Should we grab some beer?" Jill offers warmly.

"Actually, we have some. And, I didn't really work much out. Mickey and Sean requested you stay with them. I told them it's up to you. "

Mia points at Thomas and Addison, who each raise up a brown box that clinks deviance. "They're from the Heineken Brewery! The tour was amazing, I can't wait to tell you all about it." Mia slips her arm into Jill's and they saunter back to the picnic table to watch the sunset over the industrial river.

Jill's plan for preservation includes staying by Mia, drinking until she passes out(alone), and catching her flight in the morning. Still, a deeper part of her can't help but wonder. She wonders if he really does like her. With limited time on the continent, she wants to be careful not to spend too much of it worrying about men. These are her last hours, and they rightfully should be devoted to her. She decides to take control. She opts to avoid Sean and Mickey and focus on beer and campground ambiance. Besides, she has a lot of celebrating to do. She wants to celebrate the fact that she's in Amsterdam, and the fact that she's going home, and the fact that she has her Mia.

Beer flows, the group mills around, and the evening is pleasant and understated. Addison's friend, Amy, is giving Jill dry looks. Amy tries several times to flirt with Mickey, who consistently repels all her advances. This makes Jill suspect something might have happened between the two of them. Amy's tall with long wavy brown hair and deep brown eyes. She has a strange bottle in her hands and she's standing at the front of the picnic table to make a show of drinking from it.

"It's absinthe." She declares, holding it up so Mia and Jill can examine it. "Would you like to drink some with me?"

Mia declines immediately, but Jill waits to watch Amy drink before deciding if she might like to try. Amy tilts her head back, the moonlight reflecting off the elegant nape of her neck. She puts the bottle to her lips and takes a gentle pull. Jill watches in fascination as the attractive American girl's face contorts and grimaces. She grabs her stomach to try to physically stop herself from throwing back up the curious drink. She has to hold in her breathing three times, before she can stand up without grabbing onto the table. She looks at the group. No one says a word.

"I have to walk." She moans. Soon, Amy is aimlessly strolling around the dark campground. Hallucinating and amused, she continues to take small drinks from the bottle.

Mickey comes over to sit beside Jill, putting his arm around her shoulder in a friendly advance. Not the embrace of a couple, but definitely he's demonstrating his fondness for her in front of everyone. She stiffens in response. If she were invisible and no one was there to see, she would put her arm around him too. But under the inquisitive eyes of their peers, she doesn't dare. She reminds herself that she has less than fifteen hours left in Europe. The temptation isn't enough. She focuses on the value in maintaining her autonomy and dignity.

The hours fade and as they do, so does her anxiety and need to over analyze the flirting situation. Everything fails to matter, the entire trip grows fuzzy. This time and place begin to escape her, slipping through an aching grasp. The beer is doing its job, and Jill, Mia, and the men are comfortably calm. Jill can see that they aren't caught up in her time or her issues. The fact that she's leaving is purely a sweet goodbye. They would let her go tonight, and be fine with never seeing her again. She is also at peace with this, and even now, in these shrinking hours, her spirit moves forward, ahead of her, back to California. She anticipates the happiness of her return. Home where she belongs. Jill stays quiet, even her mind is still, absorbing the Zeeburg evening.

Mickey and Sean become quiet, too.

Mickey comes back from the restroom and announces to the group, "I've had too much beer. Would you like me to take your backpack to the tent, dear Jill?"

Jill nods in compliance. Mickey lifts the pack and starts to walk off into the meadow to find his way to the tent. Without a word, Sean gets up and follows. Now there are six. Mia, Jill, Thomas, Paul, Addison, and the strange American beauty on Absinthe.

Another hour passes over the courtyard, the moon hides behind thick swollen clouds. The mood is light and the telling of stories and drinking beer from green bottles keeps the group together for a little longer. Mia and Jill are huddled next to one another, sitting jovially on top of the table, their feet rest on the bench. This is the bookend. A good match to the beginning of the trip, so many nights ago.

"Are you going to make it to the airport okay tomorrow, Jill?" Mia asks with concern. Counting out the minutes she has left with her friend in her head. "Wake me, I'll go with you in the morning. All the way to the airport.

Jill smiles a long thin line, pressing her lips together with nostalgia and cheer. She would miss Mia, her manager, always organizing and restructuring her way in the world. "Okay. I would like that. We can grab breakfast together." Jill answers.

"It's a plan then. We'll save our goodbyes for tomorrow." Mia squeezes Jill's forearm.

"Count on it, tomorrow." Jill squeezes back.

The night folds in on itself and no one can manage anymore beer. Everyone has the perfect fill, enough to have a raging buzz, but not enough to throw any of it up. Everyone except Amy, who at one point starts speaking in tongues. Addison has her wrapped up in a big bear hug as she sits in his lap. She looks euphoric and happy. Jill watches her with fascination for several minutes. She sits awhile, quiet and passive, watching Mia flirt with Paul. Thomas leaves to go to bed. Jill never asks Mia for the details of her night at the camp. She basically has the primary events figured out. It appears to be that Mia and Paul are in a full blown courtship. This new romance makes Jill joyful for her friend.

Now she has to confront the part of the night she's been avoiding. It's after midnight and everyone's pushing against the edges of consciousness. Minds drift to sleepful places. Dreams call them to bed. These are the last hours of her grand adventure and the momentum of the travel and collected experiences are jamming up. All the new ideas swirl around and jumble. She holds on by her fingertips. Still, time presses down on her, the gravity of the deepest parts of the night impeding and waiting for the rest to untangle the delusion.

Jill watches the two couples cuddling at the tables, Mia with Paul and Addison with Amy. Jill looks out over the field, focusing on the little blue tent where her backpack, and Mickey, and Sean are settled. She can't delay any longer, and as nervous as she is; bravery guides her to the end of her trip: Mickey's tent.

She's going to sleep beside the clever and handsome men. Convincing herself that they would be asleep, passed out, and wouldn't even notice her next to them. She decides she can be ninja quiet, and that they were only teasing her anyways.

With a hefty sigh, she goes to the bathroom. Inside, she splashes cool water on her face. She catches a glimpse of her own reflection in the mirror. It's bright inside the bathroom, the light makes her blink. She tries to see what everyone else saw. She wants to know how she's perceived, and if it synchronizes with how she visualizes herself. She wants to be genuine and honest, and when she comes to that conclusion, Jill's mind quickly darts to the fact that she would like to sleep close to Mickey tonight. Her heart beats fast, she places her hands onto the sink, taking one last stare. A stare between her, and herself. Like a young seal plunging into an arctic water, she steps into the cool night. She walks directly to her shelter. She reasons that whatever she finds waiting for her in the tent, won't really matter. In less than nine hours, she'll be on a plane, flying to her home far away.

The picnic tables are empty. Everyone's retreated to their places of slumber.

She stands completely still, gaping at the zipper on the blue tent. She reaches down, slowly pulling it up and around to open the flap. It's so cold farther out in the meadow, perhaps because it's in such close proximity to the river. Once inside, she stumbles slightly, waiting for her eyes to adjust.

She can make out two figures in individual heaps tucked warmly into sleeping bags.

"Hello, Jill. You made it back to our tent. Did you have fun tonight?" An Irish accent whispers.

Jill jolts, startled by the greeting.

"Sorry, we didn't stay up with you." He whispers in a soft and sweet way. His voice helps Jill feel less intimidated. The kindness lures her in. "Forgive us?"

Sean speaks. "So, you're sleeping in the middle then tonight, right love?" He giggles with amusement. "Not to worry, Jill. I'm just giving you a hard time."

"Don't mind him, love. He's an arse. You can sleep over here." Mickey pats a small space on the floor of the tent in the corner, right beside him. The pat on the ground was reminiscent of the way he patted the spot on the bench beside him earlier in the day.

She's ready to cooperate with him. Anything he wants. She's tired of putting up defenses and walls over the last two weeks. She's done being tough. The invitation to curl up next to him tonight is what she wants. So she takes it.

She manages to find her sleeping bag. She pulls it out of her backpack without attracting too much attention. She lays her bag down and as fast as she can, she wiggles down into it, pushing herself against the woven structure of the little tent.

Jill skimped on her sleeping bag for the trip. It's actually a felt liner, but she decided she'd make it work. It reduced the amount of space in her backpack. Jill was right for the most part, the bag didn't use a lot of space, and it worked out fine most nights, but tonight she's freezing. Mickey and Sean settle in their bags, assimilating to the new guest in the little tent.

"Goodnight, Jill." Sean's voice calls out from within his sleeping bag. "If you need help staying warm tonight, just come over to me. I know how to keep a girl warm." He rolls to the side and mumbles, "Better than any of the men in camp."

"Goodnight, Sean." Jill retorts, feeling a little vulnerable and embarrassed.

"It's true, Jill. Sean knows how to please the ladies. Many of them cried when he left Ireland." Mickey rolls to his side.

Aaah, yes. That was a sad day. The women miss me so." Sean remarks. "Many cold women in Ireland tonight."

"Goodnight, Jill," Mickey whispers, before yawning and rolling onto his side.

"Goodnight." Jill's disappointed she can't think of something more to say. It's her last chance, and all the words have been smothered by fatigue and alcohol. Overwhelmed by the feeling of being cold, and the feeling of being beside Mickey, and the feeling of taking short light breaths, because she didn't want them to hear her out of breath, even though she feels like she is. She just surrenders to the hopelessness of herself.

She closes her eyes and lets the fact that she's okay, give her comfort. She looks forward to sleep and tomorrow. The tent is still, and she thinks both men have fallen back asleep. She doesn't move. Bothered by irony, she would have been upset if something did happen, and now she's upset that something won't.

Then, what she wishes for happens. She feels his body move in close to hers. The warmth of his heat cuts through the bitter temperature that hugs her fleece sleeping liner. The cold makes it feel natural to move close to him. Sleeping bags are peeled down enough so that two bodies can meet, and touch, and help be warm. As natural as a touch, a kiss. Mickey kisses Jill. Then another, gentle and considerate. Kissing, petting, and holding continue. Jill wants to be more present in this encounter. She's remorseful she isn't pursuing and playing with the opportunity. Part of her wants to see where this will go, how far it might escalate, and what it would mean. Something else, something firm and insistent keeps Jill back. Even though she is right there in his arms, she knows he isn't hers, and she would never be his. This depresses her. With each insincere kiss, she feels something new: Jill is sad.

It's tomorrow that drags her away from him and the fantasy. In her heart, she's already gone. She's already said goodbye to Zeeburg, and all European discoveries. Her mind is turned to the future, and in the future, she doesn't want to feel heartache. Why he was doing this, reaching out to her now, makes no sense.

He trails his fingertips over her hand and up her arm, this calms her and stirs her at the same time. She debates if a conversation needs to take place, if she needs to speak to him. Perhaps find him and connect beyond the dark tent. Should she suggest they go somewhere to explore this prospect? For whatever reason, she lies beside him at the end of a long journey. She's sad she fails to understand why he wants to be so close to her. She's afraid of the truth. He senses her resistance and gradually pulls away, back to his own sleeping bag. Eventually, Jill and Mickey fall asleep.

.　　.　　.　　.　　.

A rooster crows from somewhere down the river. He isn't the only bird awake making busy bird sounds. The sun rises and the space around the river starts to liven. Jill can hear the hum of nature outside the tent. She rolls over, trying to fit as much of her body as possible into her fleece liner bag. It's cold. She can see the form of Mickey. During the halfway point in the night he had inched his way away from Jill so he was cuddled up to Sean. All she can make out is an awkward Irish hairline peeking out from down-filled covers. She decides to stare at this for several minutes, but it doesn't provide the same exquisite sensation as his smile or his green eyes. She looks around and wonders what time it is. Her plane leaves at nine-thirty in the morning and she will need to get there early to go through customs. Jill decides her best plan of action is to rise and make a stealthy exit.

Jill silently shimmies out of her bag before crumpling it up into a ball. She stuffs it back into her backpack as she tries to strategize how to get herself and the pack out of the tent undetected. While sliding her feet into each shoe, she decides to climb backwards from the tent first, then reach in to pull her pack out second. She scans the tent, and spots her travel pouch crumpled in the corner where her shoes had been. She fumbles with it for a second, and as she lifts it, a handful of coins fall out. She stares at the coins for a second, discouraged to have to pick them all up. She looks at the men. She considers leaving the money behind. There's probably less than twenty American dollars, not enough to be bothered with having to go to a currency exchange. The men had been so kind, and helpful. They would enjoy the money. They could buy some Heineken. Then she second guesses herself. What if it's like a hooker sort of situation. Like he thinks, she's tipping him? She ponders the possibility of misinterpreting the sad pile of change on the floor of the tent. Then shakes the thought from her mind. She turns to face the door. With complete control, directing every muscle to submit to her will, she moves to the canvas flap, only glancing back at Sean and Mickey once. Mickey's head is still hidden within a blanket. Still cold, the air on the outside is even cooler than the air inside the tent. She shivers, goose bumps spring along the tops of her arms and shoulders.

She won't say goodbye, or try to steal a farewell kiss. She's done here, and just wants to throw herself into the long journey home, over the ocean. Back to the things she loves. She wants to return home and bring with her the experiences that have forged new perspectives and survival tactics. She visualizes herself walking in long strides through the San Francisco Airport, dirty and weighted by her heavy pack. She pictures the image of a worldly woman, smart and intellectual.

Outside the tent, she's free. She quickly re-zips the flap and moves across the camping field like a fox. The sly vixen that she is, going without stopping or slowing down until she reaches the bathroom. With one quick pee, and a check in the mirror, she drifts back out and up to the street to meet the sidewalk that will take her to the bus stop. Jill notices how easy the transition comes to her and she understands that over the course of her comings and goings, she somehow has gained the skills along the way to achieve self-reliance.

She looks back only once, her eyes settling on Paul and Thomas's tent. She could wake Mia, but they would probably take an hour to say goodbye. Jill assumes her friend is probably cuddling and staying warm, kept safe among her new companions. Jill also knows that Mia understands, and won't be hurt, she may even be proud. Jill gives no one in the camp the chance to say goodbye to her, and that's exactly how she likes it.

.   .   .   .   .

Jill soldiers on, entering the official doors of the international airport. She's held in customs for over an hour. She comes close to losing it when a security agent pops open the door to the compartment which houses the thirty five millimeter film from her favorite camera.

Relief floods her soul when she eventually reaches her seat on the jet plane. She won't stop until she reaches Washington. After lift-off a flight attendant makes her rounds, passing out orange frosted scones and chocolate muffins. Jill takes both. She bites into the chocolate muffin and frowns. They are crap compared to the baked confections in Europe. She decides to hold on to them for when she feels hungry. She grabs the paper sickness bag tucked into the seat in front of her. She dumps the goods inside and neatly folds down the top. She reclines and shuts her eyes. One word bounces and echoes through her soul while she sits in anticipation, "Home."

One last layover, and Jill's practically in San Francisco. She walks aimlessly through an American flight terminal, staring at magazine racks and coffee stands. Gleefully approaching her gate, she finds a few empty seats next to a young man traveling alone. He's resting in the corner of the streamlined space. The perfect place to wait. Jill's checked her pack, but her bigger camera and travel pouch are going strong, hooked over her neck like a badge of honor. When she sits down, the young man's eyes open. He gives her a half smile then looks down to the floor.

"Hi," Jill says. "Are you traveling alone?"

The boy can't avoid eye contact. He looks up with reluctance. "Yes."

"Well, where are you going?"

The boy holds his breath before he answers, "Missouri."

Jill's eyes spark with a wildness he can't decipher, "You aren't!"

"I am. Why? Are you going there, too?"

"No, no." She shakes her head, smug with humor, entertained by her own personal joke.

The young man waits for her to explain. She doesn't. Awkward tension clings to the conversation. Jill likes it. An announcement invites flyers to line up to prepare to board. Jill leans in. "I just got back from Amsterdam. Do you like skunk?" She shoves the paper bag with the muffin and scone into this lap. "Here. Have fun in Missouri."

The boy doesn't answer, looking down fearfully at the strange paper bag from Amsterdam. He remains still, watching Jill walk away.

Par la suite

It's one of those perfectly golden California days. Jill and Mia are on another trip. Only this time, just for the night, and only an hour's drive by car. They're hiking, and as the trail climbs it twists in and out of Giant Sequoia groves. The forest is dark and the ground is soft, layered with decayed pine needles. Rays of light show through the canopy, casting ethereal hues on patches of moist earth. The red bark of old trees glows in a palette that won't be found in the Louvre of Paris.

Mia walks over to a redwood with a large hollow opening inside. She goes in. She reaches up, sinking her thumb deep into the black, charred insides of the tree. She pops back out and rubs a charcoal smudge on her forehead. She walks over to Jill, lifting up her arm, placing her thumb on Jill's face. She drags her thumb all the way across the middle section of Jill's forehead. After removing her thumb, she stands back to examine her work. Mia laughs so hard she snorts. Jill laughs, too.

"Whatever, Mia! Let's hike."

They refocus and continue on their mission. They're searching for a very large, extra-old grove located beyond the reach of a trail system. The hike meanders alongside creek beds where pink mushrooms sprout and ferns fan in regal shapes. The creeks splash into deep pockets of water where little frogs sing songs about eating bugs and finding love. They're home, and it makes good sense. This is theirs, and now back in their element, they remember why they had spoken so proudly of their heritage and country. Why they're so fond, and couldn't help but boast about their good fortune to be citizens of the United States. They love this land. Embedded deep in the ancient forests of sequoia, they tap into the root of the American Heart. Blessed in wood ash they navigate through the imperial trees, talking and laughing about nothing. And, in the spirit of nothing, eventually a common subject comes to light:

"I miss our Irish boys!" Mia sighs, stepping over a few small boulders.

"I know what you mean. I just wish we could have them here. I want to show them our California!" Jill agrees, trying to step over the same boulders that Mia's just passed.

"So, Jill . . . .," Mia pauses, dragging out her inquiry.

"Yes?" Jill knows what question is coming. She's been wondering when it would be brought up.

"What happened with you and Mickey?" Mia's voice rises at the end of her question.

Jill wonders why Mia assumes it would be Mickey and not Sean.

"I don't know," Jill tries to play it off, as it she doesn't understand the question.

"Oh, come on! If you tell me, I'll tell you what Mickey said."

This proposal causes Jill to trip over a dip in the trail, knocking her off balance. She never considered Mickey would say things.

"You know, I have Sean's number, and Paul's number, if you want to get a hold of them." Mia says in a teasing voice.

Jill blushes, trying to play it cool. She's not willing to confess her crush out loud. "I don't need their numbers." Then she breaks. "What did Mickey say?"

"What happened?" Mia coaxes.

"Well, I went to bed around the same time you did, and, uh, I just got into my sleeping bag. We kissed a little and fell asleep."

Mia doesn't answer.

"So, in the morning . . . I just snuck out of the tent. I didn't even say goodbye." Jill can't help it, when she explains the last part, her voice is sad.

"Oh. Mickey told a different story." Mia's voice sounds suspiciously mischievous.

"Wait, was it about some money I left in their tent?"

"Money? I didn't hear anything about money. You left them money?"

They pick up speed, turning and snaking through the towering trees.

"Okay, what? Come on! Tell me!" Jill can't stand not knowing.

Mia starts to laugh. "I don't know if I should. I hope you won't be mad."

"Oh, wow, you have to tell me what he said now!"

Mia stops, she holds onto her side and prepares to tell Jill what he said. She resembles a comedian who's about to tell a solid gold punch line.

"What?" Jill laser focuses her eyes into Mia's.

"Mickey said you had sex, and umm then, in the middle of the night you woke up, and were so hungry you started going through the tent trying to find some food to eat." Mia has to stop, she has to get control of her laughter so she can give Jill the rest, but every time she looks at Jill with the black ash smothered across her forehead, she starts to giggle again.

Jill's silent, digesting the really unpleasant news, the betrayal from Mickey. It hurts.

"Okay, I have to tell you the rest. Mickey and Sean swear that you woke up in the middle of the night and found a can of their beans in the tent. They said you tore the lid off the can of beans and poured all the beans into your mouth like it was a can of soda." Mia starts to laugh deep with her stomach muscles. "It sort of became the camp joke. Every once in a while one of the guys would mimic you holding an invisible can of beans up to your mouth, and going aaauuuggghhh."

Mia stops laughing and looks at Jill. "Jill, did you eat their can of beans?"

Jill stands there, panicked in the middle of one of her favorite trails. Her face is redder than the redwoods. She can feel her cheeks get hot, imagining all the boys going around camp laughing at her. How could Mickey say that? Of course he would say that. They love stories. "No! I didn't eat beans, and I didn't have sex with them!" Jill's irritated, but also grateful that Mia's sharing her information.

"Oh, Jill, I'm so sorry. But, I believed them. I thought you ate the beans!" Mia starts to laugh again, holding in her stomach.

Jill turns, trying to process the joke and how she feels about it. Surprised her good friend had believed she ate the beans all these months. She let the hike move her away from the bad news. She figures if she hikes fast enough, she can hike away from the disturbing fact that Mickey and the others were laughing at her.

Mia catches up to her friend. "Hey, it's okay. It wasn't as mean at it sounds. You know how those guys love to tell crazy stories. Mickey really likes you. I can tell."

Jill stops. "He does? I mean, you think he does? Why would he say that?"

"You know those Irish guys. They say stuff. He likes you." Mia punches Jill in the arm lightly. She puts her hand up to her mouth and gestures; "aaaaauuughhhh."

Jill erupts into laughter.

"Was he a good kisser?"